A NOTE TO READERS

While Lizzie Murray and her family and friends are fictional, what happens in Boston in this story is not. It is twelve years before the Revolutionary War, but Boston's streets are already filled with violence. Angry because of increasing taxes, mobs are attacking British agents and soldiers. They burn homes and destroy property. Even people who are forced to house British soldiers are not safe from the mob's fury.

While it is easy for us to look back now and see where these events would lead, things were not so clear to King George III, Sam Adams, James Otis, or the thousands of colonists who were trying to decide the right thing to do. As we will see in this story, even individual families were not safe from the conflicts that raged through the colonies.

SISTERS IN TIME

Lizzie
and the Redcoat

STIRRINGS OF REVOLUTION IN
THE AMERICAN COLONIES

SUSAN MARTINS MILLER

BARBOUR
PUBLISHING

Lizzie
and the Redcoat

Cover design by Lookout Design Group, Inc.

Published by Barbour Publishing, Inc., P.O. Box 719, Uhrichsville, Ohio 44683, www.barbourbooks.com

Our mission is to publish and distribute inspirational products offering exceptional value and biblical encouragement to the masses.

 Member of the
Evangelical Christian
Publishers Association

Printed in the United States of America.
5 4 3 2 1

CONTENTS

CHAPTER 1
The Attack!

Lizzie loved winter.

Perched in a wing chair scooted up to the window, she pressed her face against the cold glass. The wind had blown a gentle curve of white powder against the clear pane. She studied the icy shapes that had formed on both sides of the glass. With her eyes squinted nearly shut, she tilted her head from side to side. Lizzie tried to imagine what the intricate patterns of the snowflakes might look like if they could only be larger. They might be like the spiderwebs she knocked down from the ceiling of her room, or they might be like the tatted lace her aunt Charlotte loved to make.

Lizzie had tried to learn to tat. Aunt Charlotte had been a patient teacher, but Lizzie's fingers simply would not go where they were supposed to go, and her projects always ended up being a tangled knot. She was almost twelve now. Perhaps she should try again. She would love to make a roomful of holiday lace—maybe even a whole Christmas tablecloth as a gift for her mother. A white lace tablecloth would look so festive on the long walnut table with the imported china dishes set just right.

Lizzie pushed her thick coppery hair away from her face and turned her cheek to the glass. The draft came in around the edges of the window and stirred up the fire in the front room of the Murray family home. Mama always said that the inside of the house was nearly as cold as the outside. The fire gave an especially loud snap, and Lizzie glanced at it. She loved the comfort of a roaring fire on a cold day.

Still, it was cold in the room, and Lizzie had been sitting in that chair near the window for almost an hour. She pulled her shawl snug around her shoulders and reluctantly crossed the room to warm her hands over the fire. The woodpile was getting low. At this time of year, it took so much wood to warm just the kitchen and front room of the family's home. Upstairs, in her unheated bedroom, Lizzie had learned to change clothes quickly and leap into bed.

Christmas was only a few days away. Lizzie could hardly believe that 1764 was almost over already. Mama had tried to tell her that when the years passed quickly, it meant you were growing up. Sometimes Lizzie wanted to be grown-up. She could choose her own clothes and perhaps drive her own carriage. But most of the time, growing up frightened Lizzie. Life in the colonies was changing, and if she were a grown-up, Lizzie would have to decide what she thought about everything. When it came to King George and the English Parliament, she was far too confused to know what she thought was right and what she thought was wrong.

Putting unsettling thoughts aside, Lizzie pictured the front room on Christmas Day. Soon the house would be filled with relatives and decorations and simple gifts of love. Her mother's brothers would come with their families. Uncle Blake and Aunt Charlotte would close down their carriage shop for the day and bundle up Isaac and Christopher. Uncle Philip would put a note on the door of his medical clinic telling people where he was in case of an emergency. He and Aunt Johanna and young Charity would descend enthusiastically on the Murray home.

A fire would burn in every room on Christmas. Her younger cousins would romp joyously through the house. They would all go to church together and come home for the biggest dinner of the year. Of course, this year holiday food would be harder to find than in the past. Boston was not the same as it had been a few years ago.

"Oh, there you are."

Lizzie turned toward the voice. "Were you looking for me, Mama?" Her mother had entered from the dining room.

"I thought you might like to see the quilt squares before I give them to Charlotte." Constance Murray spread two dozen carefully pieced quilt squares on and around the large chair next to the fire. A blue-and-white floral pattern emerged.

"They're beautiful, Mama," Lizzie said sincerely. "Your corners are perfect. I wish I could learn to quilt like that."

Her mother smiled. "You will. It takes years of practice."

"Aunt Johanna will love the quilt." Lizzie fingered the edge of one square and smiled faintly at the thought of her gentle aunt, married to her mother's younger brother, Philip. Lizzie was glad to have Aunt Johanna to confide in.

"I only wish Charlotte and I could have finished it in time for Christmas," Mama said.

"But Aunt Johanna's birthday is only a few weeks away," Lizzie said. "She'll have it soon enough." She looked up at her mother with a sly smile. "Do you think she suspects anything?"

"I certainly hope not." Mama started to gather up the quilt squares and stack them neatly again. "After all the hours Charlotte and I have spent on this project, I want it to be a complete surprise."

Lizzie chuckled. "I love the way Aunt Johanna holds her breath when she is surprised and doesn't know what to say."

Mama laughed, too. "Maybe that's why I like to surprise her." She offered the quilt squares to Lizzie. "Here. Why don't you take these down to your aunt Charlotte? I think she's at the carriage shop this afternoon. She's anxious to start putting the quilt together."

Lizzie looked toward the window. "But, Mama, it's cold out, and it will be dark soon."

"You have plenty of time if you just go and come directly back. Besides, I know you love the snow."

"Please, Mama, can't Joshua go?"

"Your brother is down at the print shop helping Papa. And I have to stay here with Emmett and Olivia. Don't be so contrary. It is not becoming to a young lady."

Lizzie heard the firmness in her mother's voice and knew she would have to go out whether she liked it or not.

She did love the snow—her mother was right about that. And the walk to Wallace Coach and Carriage Company, owned by Uncle Blake and Aunt Charlotte, was not a long one. A crisp, bright winter day was Lizzie's favorite kind of weather, and Mama knew that. But it was no longer fun to walk around the streets of Boston. Lizzie much preferred to stay indoors and imagine that all was well.

"Wear your warmest cloak, and you should be fine," Mama said. "Tuck the quilt squares underneath to keep them dry."

"Yes, Mama," Lizzie said softly and went to fetch her cloak.

Outside, she took a deep breath and looked around. The street where the Murrays lived was a quiet one. The families who lived there were proud of their homes. They had worked hard to build their houses and make them every bit as comfortable as the homes newcomers spoke of having left in England. Goods came into the colonies from everywhere, but mostly from England. Business had been good for many years.

That was changing now. Some people were so angry with King George and the Parliament in England that they refused to buy anything that came from England. And Parliament disapproved of the colonies bringing in too many goods from anywhere else.

Lizzie turned a corner and started walking in the direction of Boston Harbor. Wallace Coach and Carriage was near the harbor. Lizzie knew that many people thought Aunt

Charlotte had no business working at the carriage shop. But Charlotte was independent enough to do as she pleased, and Uncle Blake seemed to appreciate the help. Lizzie admired Aunt Charlotte's fire as much as she admired Aunt Johanna's gentleness.

Around the next corner, Lizzie's heart quickened at the sight of the British soldiers. They were standing guard outside the Customs House, the brick building where the king's treasury in Boston was kept. There were two guards, one on either side of the doorway. They stood silently still, with their red coats properly buttoned and their muskets always ready. Their white collars were so stiff they could hardly move their heads. Lizzie kept her eyes fixed on the street ahead of her and focused on putting one foot in front of the other just to keep moving. If she had gone the long way around, she might have avoided the soldiers. But it was too late now. Beneath her cloak, her fingers gripped the quilt squares that had brought her out on this day.

Lizzie hated the feeling she got in her stomach whenever she saw British soldiers on duty. British soldiers had been in Boston her whole life, but they had always been small in number with pleasant responsibilities. They had worked alongside the colonists for the good of both England and the colonies. Now, it seemed that they were everywhere, and they were here to do what King George wanted them to do, not what the Bostonians wanted.

Even the townspeople could not agree about what was best for the colonies. In the past, no one had seemed to mind the soldiers. Now, everyone argued about whether the soldiers should stay in Boston or be packed up and sent home on the next boat to England. Lizzie had heard her uncles dispute that question many times.

Not so long ago, Boston had been bubbling with energy. The harbor had been filled with boats, and everyone in town had been curious to see the new items they brought in. Books, fine furniture, and clothing had come from Europe, and the colonists had felt they were as much a part of life in England as if they still lived there.

At the same time, Boston had become a real city. Schools and newspapers—including Papa's print shop—had flourished. Carpenters were kept busy filling orders for furniture and equipment for the outlying farms. Craftsmen had worked on jewelry, dishes, and decorations for the homes of Boston's upper class. Blacksmiths kept shoes on hundreds of horses. Women from the other colonies traveled to Boston to see what the new fashions were. Church bells rang to remind the people to worship the God who had blessed them. The streets had been filled with horses and carriages as people came into town to shop and visit and exchange information.

Lizzie had loved living in Boston when so much was going on. She could go into Mr. Osgood's shop for a sweet treat or to the dressmaker's shop to see sketches of the new clothes from Europe. But those shops were closed now. The molasses that Mr. Osgood used in many of his sweets had gotten too expensive because of new taxes, and the dressmaker had taken an independent spirit and refused to follow the fashions from England.

Lizzie did not understand very much about the Seven Years' War. She knew that the colonies had fought alongside England against the French. At the end of the war, some of the land they had been fighting over was given to France.

From reading the small newspaper that her father published, Lizzie also knew that King George in England was not happy with the colonies. He thought that they did not help enough during the Seven Years' War and that they should have done much more to help the British troops. More of the men should have fought, the king thought, and those who did not could have given food and supplies more willingly. The Seven Years' War—which had lasted for most of Lizzie's life—had drained the treasury of England. The relationship between the colonies and their mother country was changed forever. Now King George seemed determined to control the colonies with an iron hand. So the soldiers were everywhere. Boston was still full of energy, but it was an angry energy, filled with dread of things to come.

Lizzie was past the soldiers now and could breathe more easily. Her brother Joshua, who was two years older than she, teased her about how nervous the soldiers made her. He liked to remind her that their own family had come from England and Ireland. "Maybe those boys outside the Customs House are our distant cousins," Joshua would say. "I think the red jackets are a bit odd, but I'm not afraid of the men who wear them."

16

Lizzie shuddered. The wind blew through her cloak. Now that she was down the street a few yards, she glanced back over her shoulder at the soldiers. They had not changed position. They seemed not to even notice the biting wind. No matter what Joshua said, the British soldiers made Lizzie nervous. Their presence meant that things were not going well in Boston. With Christmas just around the corner, Lizzie yearned to feel free of the foreboding presence that followed her everywhere she went.

Suddenly Lizzie was pulled off balance from behind! She tried to scream, but a firm hand on her mouth stifled the sound.

CHAPTER 2

The Customs Agent

Lizzie lost her balance and fell backward, straight into the chest of her attacker. He swung her around and lifted her feet off the ground, spinning her around three times. Her arms and feet flailed against the empty air. When she landed, she kicked backward as hard as she could until she struck something solid—a shin.

"Ouch!" With a grunt that revealed his pain, he released Lizzie immediately.

Once free, she started to run up the street—until she looked over her shoulder and saw the identity of her attacker.

"Joshua Murray! You frightened me half to death." She charged at her fourteen-year-old brother, who merely grinned back at her. He was amused by her anger. "Why in the world would you do such a thing?"

Joshua caught her wrists before she could strike him. "I'm sorry. I couldn't help myself. I saw you walking past the sentries and thought it would be a shame to let all that fear go to waste. You could not even look at their faces."

"What does that matter?" Lizzie asked indignantly. "I did not come out in the cold to visit with soldiers." She turned and began walking again.

"They wouldn't hurt you, you know." Joshua fell into step beside her.

"I don't want to talk about it."

"You're just a girl. You're not a soldier or a militiaman. You are no threat to them."

"I said I didn't want to talk about it." Lizzie speeded up her steps.

"Where are you going?"

"To the carriage shop. Mama has finished her quilt squares for Aunt Johanna, and Aunt Charlotte is going to put them together."

"I'll come along," Joshua said. "I always like visiting the carriage business."

"Doesn't Papa need you?" Lizzie asked.

"I'm finished for today at the print shop."

"Well, if you must, you may come along." Lizzie gave her brother a harsh look. Inwardly, however, she was glad to have Joshua with her. Not only was he bigger and stronger than she was, but he was not afraid. Nothing that had happened in Boston in recent months made him avoid being outside. When she was with Joshua, Lizzie felt less afraid herself.

Soon Boston Harbor came into view. The sun glinted off the water as the waves lapped into the protection of the half-frozen harbor.

"I love coming down here," Joshua said. He slowed his steps to gaze at the mass of boats and docks before them. He braced himself against a railing and looked directly out over the water. "Don't you ever wonder about all the places those boats have been, all the things that the crews have seen?"

Lizzie shrugged. "It's enough for me just to see the things they bring back. Except they don't bring much anymore."

Ships lined the docks, but the mighty masts were down on many of them. Only three ships were being unloaded. December was a difficult time to sail the ocean, and some of the shippers and other business owners had lost a lot of business because people in the colonies were refusing to contribute to the king's well-being by purchasing goods from England.

"Uncle Blake seems to be keeping busy enough at the shop. He has more business all the time. Just last week, seven more coaches were brought to him for repair, not to mention the orders he already had for new carts and carriages."

Lizzie nodded. "I think I heard Aunt Charlotte say something about that."

"When I'm sixteen, I'm going to ask Papa to let me work with Uncle Blake," Joshua said. "At least for a little while."

"I thought you were going to work at the print shop with Papa when you finish school."

"There is plenty of time for both." Joshua's eyes brightened. "I wonder what the cargo is on the ships that just arrived—and whether Uncle Blake is paying taxes on the goods he receives."

"Uncle Blake runs an honest business," Lizzie said with certainty. She gestured that they should resume their walk.

"I'm not sure anyone is completely honest anymore," Joshua said. He let his fingers trail lightly along the rail as he walked. "I've heard a lot of rumors about smuggling lately. Papa even has a story about it in the newspaper."

"Smuggling?" Lizzie asked. "What does the story say? Does Papa think it's true?"

"You know Papa. He likes to report the facts and let people make up their own minds."

"What about you?"

Joshua shrugged. "Who knows? Parliament is enforcing the Sugar Act, and the customs agents are watching all the ships carefully. I know Uncle Blake does not agree with the Sugar Act. He says it will cost everyone a lot of money in taxes."

Will I never escape danger? Lizzie wondered. She was on a simple errand to take quilt squares to her aunt, and she found herself suspecting her uncle of breaking the laws of England.

They approached the big wooden door to Wallace Coach and Carriage. Joshua and Lizzie had grown up visiting this office. Blake Wallace had inherited Wallace Coach from his uncle, Randolph Wallace, after an apprenticeship and a time of learning to run the business. Blake had expanded the company—and the name—after several years, adding newer models of carriages like the phaeton and the landau. Wallace Coach and Carriage had flourished under his direction and was quite the modern business now.

Joshua pushed open the door, and they went in. A man

in a long gray coat stood across from Uncle Blake's desk, talking intently.

"He looks angry," Lizzie whispered.

"Don't mind him," Joshua said. "He's just the customs agent."

Lizzie's eyes widened. "The customs agent? Is Uncle Blake already in trouble?"

Joshua put a finger to his lips to hush Lizzie and steered her toward the back of the office. Aunt Charlotte stood in the doorway to the back room. She wiggled her finger to say they should join her. Her two small sons, six and eight years old, poked their heads around her billowing skirts to try to see what was happening in the outer office. Charlotte gently pushed their heads back.

"What's going on?" Lizzie whispered as Aunt Charlotte herded them into the back room.

"The customs agent thinks Blake is evading the required taxes on goods for the business."

Lizzie caught her breath. *Is Joshua right? Is Uncle Blake defying the king?*

"I knew it!" Joshua said victoriously. "Uncle Blake is not going to let the British push him around."

"You know no such thing," Aunt Charlotte said sternly. "What your uncle does with his business is no concern of yours, and I'll thank you not to spread rumors that you know nothing about."

"Yes, ma'am," Joshua said. He said no more, but Lizzie could see in Joshua's eyes that he still believed Uncle Blake was deliberately disobeying the king's laws.

"I'm sure you did not come to watch this little show," Aunt Charlotte said. "Has your mother sent you?"

"Oh! I completely forgot!" Lizzie reached under her cloak and brought out the quilt squares. "Mama sent me with these. I'm afraid I've wrinkled them a bit." She glared at Joshua. "I got a little nervous walking over here."

Aunt Charlotte set the squares on a table and began smoothing them out. "These will do just fine. Your mother is one of the best quilters I know." She began moving the squares around in different arrangements. Without looking up, she spoke. "Isaac Wallace, you mind me. Stay in this room."

Little Isaac moaned and stepped back from the doorway. Lizzie smiled to herself. Like her own mother, Aunt Charlotte knew what her children were doing even when she could not see them.

The sounds from the outer office grew louder.

"I assure you, Mr. Wallace," the customs agent said, nearly shouting by now, "you will face consequences for your actions!"

"With all due respect, sir," Uncle Blake replied calmly, "you have not specified any actions worthy of consequences."

"See," Lizzie whispered to Joshua, "Uncle Blake is not doing anything illegal."

"That is not what he said," Joshua responded. "Maybe the customs agent hasn't figured it all out yet. He needs more information to charge Uncle Blake with wrongdoing."

Lizzie pressed her lips together and looked through the doorway at her uncle. Could Joshua be right?

Joshua quietly stepped into the outer office and leaned casually against the wall.

"Joshua! What are you doing?" Lizzie used the loudest whisper she could without drawing attention to herself.

"Just standing here," he answered. But he slid along the wall a few steps at a time.

"Boys, get back," Aunt Charlotte said to her sons.

"But Joshua is out there," the older one protested.

"Pay no attention to Joshua."

But Aunt Charlotte did pay attention to Joshua. Her eyes followed his movement around the outer office. Lizzie and her little cousins peeked out to watch, too. Slowly and silently, Joshua inched his way around the room until he was squarely behind the customs agent. Lizzie and Aunt Charlotte looked at each other and chuckled as quietly as they could. They knew what was coming next.

The customs agent's white powdered wig jiggled humorously as he shook his head at Uncle Blake. Behind him, Joshua scowled and shook his head from side to side in a comically exaggerated motion.

"It would behoove you to be honest with me, Mr. Wallace," the agent said. "I have the full authority of the king behind me. Do not try to deceive me."

Joshua mouthed an echo of everything the angry man said.

"I assure you, Mr. Byles," Uncle Blake said, "it is not

necessary for you to be so curious about my activities. Wallace Coach and Carriage is a family business that has been operating for decades in full cooperation of British law. We did not organize ourselves simply to frustrate the king."

"Don't make fun of me!" Mr. Byles shouted, shaking a finger at Uncle Blake.

Joshua shook his finger in a stern gesture.

"I can assure you that if I find any evidence to support my suspicions, you will find yourself in serious trouble." Mr. Byles set his hands on his hips and glared at Uncle Blake.

Joshua did the same.

"Look at Joshua!" one of the boys exclaimed. "He's funny!"

"Hush!" Aunt Charlotte said. "Pay him no mind." But her eyes caught Lizzie's and twinkled.

"I am fully aware of the consequences of evading taxes, Mr. Byles," Uncle Blake said. The slightest of smiles formed on his lips as he caught Joshua's eye. Joshua grinned back at his uncle.

"I would suggest you take that smirk off your face, Mr. Wallace. I do not take kindly to being ridiculed."

Joshua stuck out his lower lip and shook his head seriously.

Blake resumed a sober expression. "Of course not, Mr. Byles. I would not think of ridiculing you."

Mr. Byles huffed in disgust. "I can think of no reason

why I should believe you," he said, "but I do have other business to attend to this afternoon."

"I am a fair man, Mr. Byles, and I understand the needs of government. I make no effort to avoid a reasonable tax."

"I can assure you that you have not seen the last of me." The agent thrust one arm up in the air to emphasize his point.

Joshua did the same.

"You are welcome to visit Wallace Coach and Carriage at any time, Mr. Byles. I trust the remainder of your day will pass pleasantly."

The customs agent turned around abruptly. Joshua immediately brought his hands down to his sides and smiled politely.

"What are you doing here?" Mr. Byles demanded.

"I have come to visit my uncle, sir," Joshua replied respectfully.

"Why did you not speak up?"

"I did not wish to disturb your conversation, sir."

"Your mother has brought you up well," Mr. Byles declared. Then he pushed past Joshua and left the shop.

"Joshua, you were wonderful," Uncle Blake said, grabbing his nephew by the shoulders. "I don't know how you can do that without bursting out in laughter."

Aunt Charlotte came out of the back room and collapsed into a wooden desk chair, laughing. Lizzie and the boys followed her out.

"Cousin Joshua, you are so funny!" Both of the boys

started making faces and shaking their fingers at each other.

"Some might think you are a disrespectful boy," Aunt Charlotte cautioned, "but it was an amusing sight."

Lizzie was laughing, too. The whole family loved to watch Joshua's impressions—even when he made fun of some of *them*.

But as she laughed, Lizzie remembered some of her uncle's words. He had not come right out and denied that he was cheating the king out of any taxes he owed. Obviously Mr. Byles was convinced he had good reason to suspect Uncle Blake. Lizzie wanted to believe her uncle was doing the right thing, but she was not sure what to think. *Does Uncle Blake feel that taxes are wrong?* Lizzie wondered. *Is he in danger?*

CHAPTER 3

The Argument on Christmas Day

Carefully, precisely, Lizzie set the china plate perfectly between the fork and knife. Then she adjusted the crystal goblet ever so slightly until she was satisfied that the place setting was exactly right. She wanted the table to be perfect for Christmas dinner. Satisfied with the first place setting, she moved on to the next. Before she was finished, she would make her way around the long walnut table covered with a white damask tablecloth until all fifteen place settings were perfectly lined up. As she surveyed the table, she imagined the family gathered around it. There would be her parents, with Joshua and Olivia and Emmett. Uncle Blake and Aunt Charlotte would be there also, with Isaac and Christopher. And Uncle Philip, Aunt Johanna, and cousin Charity would complete the gathering.

Lizzie straightened a narrow ladder-back chair until it was perfectly lined up with the place setting before it. She paused to pick up a plate and admire it. She had always loved the delicate pink-and-green flower pattern. Seeing it and holding the plate made Lizzie feel a mysterious connection to her great-grandmother, who had received these dishes as a wedding present. Two of the plates had slight nicks, but none of the pieces had been broken. Lizzie likened the dishes to her family—they were not perfect people, but they were a family, bound together by love passed down for generations.

"Can I help you?" The request came from six-year-old Olivia, Lizzie's sister. Olivia was not exactly known for her gentle touch. She was a rambunctious child, fearful of nothing and always ready to try something new. Lizzie winced inwardly at the thought of Olivia touching their great-grandmother's china. Yet she did not want to hurt Olivia's feelings. She remembered how proud she had felt the first time she was allowed to help set the table.

"How about if we do it together?" Lizzie proposed.

Happily, Olivia agreed, and with one of Lizzie's hands on Olivia's shoulder and the other firmly holding the plate, they laid the next place setting.

"I helped, I helped!" Olivia cried and scampered off to the front room to brag to her cousins.

Lizzie smiled and turned back to her task. But she was soon interrupted again.

"I want to help!" announced her cousin Isaac.

"Me, too!" said his brother Christopher.

"I'll help," said five-year-old Charity, Uncle Philip and Aunt Johanna's daughter.

Lizzie's youngest brother, five-year-old Emmett, said nothing but looked up at her with his wide dark eyes. Lizzie could never resist Emmett when he looked like that. She was faced with three little boys and a girl who all wanted to help set the table with china and crystal.

Isaac reached for the stack of plates, and Lizzie stopped him just in time.

"I'll tell you what," she said. "You can all help, but you have to take turns."

"Me first! Me first!" Isaac and Christopher said, almost together.

Lizzie looked at Emmett. She knew he would never insist on having the first turn. Emmett and Lizzie understood each other. Despite almost seven years' difference in their ages, they were more like each other than anyone else in the Wallace or Murray families.

"Let's start with the youngest," Lizzie said as she took Emmett's hand. Systematically, she helped them all set a plate on the table in the proper spot: first Emmett, then Charity, then Isaac, and finally Christopher.

Satisfied, the little ones scurried away to return to their play. As Lizzie watched them go, she wondered what was going on in their minds. Although the older boys wore the long breeches of adult men, they were only children. Did they feel the sense of danger and fear that she felt? Did they know that the unrest in the streets of Boston was not normal? Lizzie comforted herself with the thought that they were young enough to fill their days and thoughts only with playing harder and learning the letters of the alphabet.

Lizzie had worked her way from one end of the table to

the other. The voices of her father and her uncles, sitting near the fireplace in the next room, filled her ears.

". . .has got to realize that it is unreasonable to expect that the people of the colonies will not want to move west," said Uncle Blake. "I cannot imagine what madness the king has fallen into to make him declare it illegal to settle any farther west than the Appalachian divide."

"I'm sure that is only for the time being," said Uncle Philip, the soft-spoken doctor.

"I should think so," said Lizzie's father, Duncan Murray. "There is an entire continent awaiting settlement—land for farms and towns. The people will not wait long."

"They are not waiting even now," said Uncle Blake. "Settlers had already started pushing west before this crazy rule came from London."

"But there are no real towns," said Papa, "no schools, no shops."

"You are right about that," Uncle Blake responded, "but those things will come. When enough people have settled and begun farming, they will organize themselves into communities and resist Parliament and the king."

"I'm afraid you are right," Papa agreed. "It would take a great many soldiers to stop the westward flow." He looked down into the mug of hot tea he held in his hand while he pondered the issue.

Through the doorway, Lizzie looked from her father to Uncle Blake to Uncle Philip, who had not said very much. Uncle Philip usually said little. He did not always agree with his older brother Blake, but it seemed to Lizzie that he would rather remain silent than cause conflict.

"Joshua tells me you had a visit from a customs agent," Papa said to Uncle Blake.

Uncle Blake chuckled. "It was nothing serious, I assure you. Ezra Byles is making regular rounds at all the shops and businesses near the harbor. He never comes right out and says what he thinks. I don't believe he has any real evidence of anything that he suspects."

"No doubt he is simply trying to frighten people into obeying the regulations from Parliament."

"Well, he does not frighten me, and I daresay he does not frighten Joshua, either. You should have seen him. He was magnificent!"

Papa smiled. "Someday those imitations are going to get him into trouble."

Uncle Blake returned to the subject of Parliament. "The colonies have always contributed to the needs of the empire. We have been a hardworking lot, and the Crown has reaped the benefit of our efforts. We've educated our children right from the start. We have our own newspapers and colleges. We've governed ourselves peaceably with our own houses of assembly. We have no need for the interference of Parliament in our affairs."

"The colonies still belong to the Crown," Uncle Philip reminded his brother. "If Isaac or Christopher told you that they did not need you any longer, I'm sure you would set them straight. They are still your sons."

"Ah, yes, but when they have grown, they may do as they please. The colonies have matured. We are not the frail, fledgling group that landed at Plymouth."

Lizzie sighed as she turned back toward the table and picked up another goblet. When Uncle Blake spoke, what he said made sense. But when Uncle Philip spoke, what he said made sense, too. The two brothers did not agree with each other, yet Lizzie was drawn to both sides of the question. She thought of herself as English, yet she had never seen London and probably never would. Her mother's family had landed in Plymouth almost 150 years before, and they didn't have any contact with the distant relatives who still lived there. Her life in the colonies was busy and full. Lizzie loved living in Boston and did not feel that she lacked anything because she had not been to London.

"Perhaps," Uncle Philip said, "the problem is not so much what Parliament is doing as it is how they are going about it."

"What do you mean?" her father asked.

"Even independent-minded colonists consider themselves loyal subjects of the king," Uncle Philip explained. "We can understand that the Seven Years' War took a heavy toll on the Crown's treasury. Perhaps if Parliament had not been so heavy-handed in the way it announced the Sugar Act, people would not disagree with it."

Uncle Blake shook his head vigorously. "No, Philip, I don't think so. We did our best to come to the aid of England during the war, and Parliament has all but ignored the contribution we made in winning the war. Parliament is treating us like we have been naughty children."

Lizzie smoothed a napkin that she had already smoothed a dozen times. It was impossible for her to judge who was right.

"I don't know what to make of it all, but I do know one thing," her father said thoughtfully. "Parliament and the colonies cannot continue this bickering for much longer without consequences. Men like Sam Adams have nearly reached their limits."

"Adams is a man of vision," Uncle Blake said.

"Adams is a man itching to stir up trouble," Uncle Philip said, disagreeing. "He's been in my clinic, spinning his stories about what is to become of the colonies."

"No matter what you think of him," Papa said, "he is a man to be reckoned with."

With a lump in her throat, Lizzie balanced herself against the ladder-back chair.

"The table looks lovely!"

At the sound of Aunt Johanna's gentle voice, Lizzie turned her attention away from the conversation in the next room and focused once more on the table.

Aunt Johanna laid one hand on Lizzie's shoulder. "No one lays a table as nicely as you do, Lizzie."

"I had some help," Lizzie said.

"So Charity told me. You are so patient with the little ones. Everything is beautiful."

"Thank you. The tablecloth needs mending. I think

Mama would like a new one, but. . ."

"Yes, I know," Johanna said softly. "It's hard to find anything in the shops now."

"Mama said she had to make all sorts of substitutions for Christmas dinner. She couldn't find anything she wanted, and she wouldn't buy any of the things that came from England."

"I know. We tried shops all over Boston."

"I'm so glad Mama has kept this china," Lizzie said. "It helps me remember what Christmas was like when I was little, before all of this started." She turned her head back toward the men.

"Have you been listening?"

Lizzie nodded.

Aunt Johanna sighed. "I would love to tell you not to be concerned about anything you have heard and that everything is going to be all right. I would love to promise that by next Christmas everything will be the way you want it to be. But I can't."

"I know," Lizzie murmured.

"Many of the things that people are angry about started a long time ago. But you were too young to be concerned with politics and loyalties. Now you're growing up. You understand more."

"I'm not sure I like it," Lizzie said as she pushed a chair in neatly under the table. "Aunt Johanna, can I tell you a secret?"

"I hope you will."

"It's not really a secret. Joshua already knows."

"What does he know?"

Lizzie looked down at her hands. "That I'm frightened. All the time."

"What are you frightened of?"

"I'm not sure. . . . Everything, I guess. I'm afraid something bad is going to happen. Something bad will happen to somebody in the family. I hate thinking about it, but it's always in my mind."

"Do you think you can stop something bad from happening?"

Lizzie shook her head. "That's the problem. I want to stop it, but how can I? I don't even know what it is."

"Who could stop it?" Aunt Johanna probed.

Lizzie shrugged. "God, I guess. But I don't know if He will. He has already let a lot of bad things happen."

Aunt Johanna sighed. "These are not easy questions, Lizzie, so I will not give you easy answers. But remember who truly is in charge."

"What do you mean?"

"Is King George in charge?"

"Well, he thinks he is, but a lot of people don't agree."

"Is Sam Adams in charge?"

"He might like to be, but he's not."

"Think about who is in charge, Lizzie, and find your peace there."

Before Lizzie could press Aunt Johanna further, they both jumped at the sound of a crash above them.

Aunt Johanna rolled her eyes. "That would be Emmett and Charity jumping off the bed again. I've told them a hundred times not to do that." She gathered her billowing skirts and turned to go inspect the damage.

CHAPTER 4

The Mob

The temperatures rose, and the ice on the pond where Lizzie had taken Olivia and Emmett to slide around during the harsh winter months melted. The heavy snows of January and February gave way to the rains of March and April. The grass, brown and brittle during the winter, once again sprang up thick and green.

As much as Lizzie loved the winter, she loved the spring even more. She dropped her satchel of books in the grass and threw herself down beside it. She had had a hard time paying attention in school that day. Every time she glanced out the window and saw the clouds pushed along by the breeze, she wanted to be outside watching them. At last the clock had struck three, and the teacher had dismissed the class. Lizzie would have to work on her arithmetic after supper, but for now, she wanted to gaze at the sky and imagine.

What did she imagine? People always wanted to know. Anything and everything. That was her answer. She would imagine the clouds were exotic animals she had never seen or mansions she would never live in. And sometimes, lately, she would imagine that the clouds were British soldiers sailing across the ocean, back to their homeland. And she would imagine that there was peace in the colonies.

Lizzie lingered in the grass outside the school as long as she dared. Papa was expecting her at the print shop to help with errands. She did not want to be scolded. So reluctantly, she pulled herself to her feet, picked up her satchel, and began the walk. By now the other children were far ahead of her, and she could at least be alone with her thoughts.

When she came to the town square, though, something was not right. Far too many people were gathered for the middle of the afternoon. Merchants who should have been busy in their shops were standing in little groups discussing something intently. The blacksmiths had left their fires, the carpenters had left their hammers, and the tailor had left his cloth. What could possibly have brought everyone out on a spring afternoon in the middle of the week? With a knot in her stomach, Lizzie quickened her steps and hurried to the print shop.

She could hardly get in the door. Inside the print shop were nearly as many people as she had seen on the square.

"Papa?" she called, but she knew he could not possibly hear her over the din of voices that filled the room.

She raised her eyes to the top of the printing press that rose from the floor and was bolted to the ceiling. Usually the huge beams of the press were the first thing she saw when she entered the shop. It was an enormous structure, and when she was six she had insisted that her father explain to her how it worked. She wanted to know everything about the iron workings inside the wooden frame, the metal that was cast into molds and pressed onto the paper that her father printed.

Today, though, she could hardly see the press—only the top where it rose above the heads of the tallest people in the room. But Lizzie could see enough to know that the press was not moving. This was the busiest time of day for the print shop. The afternoon newspaper should be stacking up on the tray, and the smell of fresh ink should be filling the room. Yet the press was still. People liked to read the newspaper, but very few ever visited the shop where it was printed. Something was very strange.

"Papa!" Lizzie called out again, louder.

"Over here, Lizzie!" The voice that spoke her name cut through the din of the crowd, and she turned her head toward it. Joshua was gesturing that she should come stand beside him along one wall.

Getting through the crowd was not easy. Lizzie had to squeeze past elbows in motion and brush against swishing full skirts. No one seemed to notice her. Along the way she caught snatches of conversation.

"This is illegal!"

"Parliament has gone too far this time!"

"The colonies should act now! We can't let them steal from us like this!"

Finally Lizzie managed to reach her older brother. "What has happened?" she asked breathlessly. "What is going on?"

"The Stamp Act," Joshua answered.

"You mean the Sugar Act," Lizzie corrected. "But that's not new."

"No, I mean the Stamp Act. Parliament passed it in March. Only now has the message reached the colonies."

Lizzie leaned against the wall and let her shoulders sag.

"What does it mean?" she asked.

"I'm not sure about all the details yet," Joshua said. He almost had to shout to be heard over the crowd. "But I think it means that people have to pay for a stamp to put on papers."

"What kind of papers?"

"Any kind of paper. Legal documents, newspapers, almanacs. Just about everything."

"So why are all these people here? What does Papa have to do with it?"

"They want to know if he is going to charge more for the newspaper and the other things he prints. But most of all, they want to know if he is going to print a story against the Stamp Act."

"Papa always tries to be fair in the stories he prints." Lizzie had always admired her father's sense of fairness, but she was beginning to wonder if it would get him in trouble.

"These people are not concerned with what is fair," Joshua said. "They are angry."

"I can see that!" Lizzie said, her voice rising to be heard above the crowd. "Were all these people in the shop when you got here after school?"

Joshua nodded. "Most of them. I don't think Papa knows I'm here yet."

The crowd pushed forward toward the printing press. The door opened, and still more people entered.

Lizzie and Joshua squeezed themselves up against the wall and listened.

"Duncan, do you understand what this means?" one man shouted, shaking his fist.

"Of course I do. This will impact my business more than you know." Duncan Murray stood on a stool trying to calm the crowd. He shook his head. "Imagine, every paper I print with a stamp on it means I have to collect more money from all of you. I don't like it any more than the rest of you."

"Then what are you going to do about it?"

"I'm going to report the facts," Lizzie's father said solidly, "so that everyone will know exactly what the law is and what it means for them."

"We already know what it means, Duncan," another man called out. "It means that Parliament is trying to squeeze more money out of us."

"Yes," said another, "and this time they are taking money that ought to stay in the colonies. Take your business, for example, Duncan. You own and operate this business completely within Massachusetts. Why should a penny of your earnings leave the colonies to go into the treasury of the king?"

Papa held up his hand and shook his head. "I didn't say

I agreed with the law. I simply said I was going to report the facts."

"Make sure you report all the facts!" Ezra Byles, the customs agent, shoved his way through the crowd and stood before Duncan Murray. "Make sure that you report the true condition of the king's treasury. The Seven Years' War was fought at a dear price, and the colonies were greedy, stingy, and uncooperative. Be sure to report that fact!"

"Stick to your job, Byles." The voice sounded aggravated. "Don't you bother enough people down at the harbor?"

"Who let that redcoat in here?" demanded a gruff voice.

The crowd began to murmur the question over and over again.

Lizzie nudged her brother. "Why would Mr. Byles come into a shop full of people angry at Parliament? Doesn't he know these people don't like him?"

Joshua laughed. "Ezra Byles thinks that just because he says, 'The king said so,' everyone will be happy to obey. Maybe his job is going to include collecting the stamp taxes now, too."

Lizzie saw her father raise his hands above the crowd.

"Mr. Byles is free to come and go as he pleases," Papa said. "He has a right to his opinion just like the rest of us."

"Is that so? If he can come and go freely, then why cannot we do the same? Why should we pay a tax that we have not chosen?"

"We are still subjects of the king," another voice said.

"We have a duty to obey this law, regardless of whether we agree with it."

"Balderdash!"

"Nonsense!"

"Another redcoat!"

"I never suspected Duncan Murray of being a redcoat!"

Lizzie gasped and looked at Joshua. Her father was being called a redcoat, one of the meanest terms anyone in Boston ever used. *How can anyone question his loyalty to the colonies?*

"Silence!" Duncan Murray shouted above the crowd. "I realize many of you disagree with this law. But it is the law of England, and we are part of England. If you want to change the law, you must take the right steps. Shouting at Mr. Byles is not going to change the law."

Lizzie's back tensed. She knew that tone in her father's voice well. He was reaching the limit of his patience.

"I want to know one more thing, Duncan," said the man who had started the whole discussion. "If an agent of the king comes to your shop and asks you to print stamps to put on legal documents, will you print the stamps?"

The room hushed. Everyone wanted to know the answer to that question. Lizzie froze, her mouth half open.

"I will not answer that question one way or another right now," Lizzie's father said. "I have not been asked to print stamps, and I may never be asked to print stamps. Now, please, I have a newspaper to print, and it is late already. Please let me get back to work." He hopped off the stool, turned his back to the crowd, and began loading paper into the press.

"I think we have some more issues to talk about," someone said.

"Not here, you don't," Papa said, wiping his hands on his leather apron. "This is a private print shop, not a public assembly hall." He lifted another stack of paper and fit the corners squarely in the metal tray. He did not look up at the crowd again.

Gradually the crowd broke up. At first they simply backed away from the press so it could be operated. Glancing at him every few seconds, they talked among themselves in low tones. But then Ezra Byles left. When they realized that the object of their opposition was gone and that Duncan Murray truly was not going to discuss the issue further, others started to drift out the door.

In a few minutes, Joshua and Lizzie were alone with their father. They looked at each other, unsure whether or not they should speak to him. Slowly they walked toward the press.

"Let me help you, Papa," Joshua said.

"I'll get the ink ready," Lizzie offered.

Papa opened his arms to his children, and they accepted his embrace. "I'm sorry if I seemed angry. I did not know you were here."

"We saw everything, Papa," Joshua said.

Papa handed Joshua a paper. "Here is a copy of the Stamp Act. You can read it for yourself."

"Are you frightened, Papa?" Lizzie asked.

Her father gave her a squeeze before answering. "Not frightened, exactly. But I am uncertain about what will happen now. Parliament has pushed the people too far this time." He turned to his son. "Joshua, from now on I want you to walk with Lizzie after school. Take her straight home or bring her here. I don't want her out on the street alone."

"Then you are afraid, Papa!" Lizzie cried.

"I'm just being careful," he replied.

"Papa?"

"Yes, Lizzie?"

"Will there be another war?"

Papa shook his head. "I can't believe anyone wants a war, Lizzie. We just have to straighten out a few wrinkles in the relationship between England and the colonies."

"So, no war?"

"No war."

CHAPTER 5

Sam Adams's Speech

"But are you absolutely sure of that?"

Lizzie listened carefully to see how her classmate would answer the teacher's question.

"Yes, sir." Sixteen-year-old Daniel Taylor answered quite confidently. He stood next to his seat as he spoke, and his eyes blazed with conviction. "I have no doubt that England needs the colonies more than the colonies need England. The king recognizes this fact, and that is why he is so eager to make the colonies submit to his will, even when his actions make no sense."

"And you think the Stamp Act makes no sense?" the teacher challenged.

"None whatsoever," Daniel said. Voices around the classroom murmured in agreement. Only a few days had passed since news of the Stamp Act had reached Boston. Already the city was polarized. Loyalists supported the king and Parliament. Patriots found that their loyalties to the colonies ran deeper than their loyalties to England. It seemed that people talked of little besides the Stamp Act. Every newspaper or flier Lizzie's father printed was sold almost immediately. People could not seem to get enough information. And most people Lizzie overheard agreed with Daniel Taylor that the stamp tax made no sense.

"Let's suppose," the teacher said thoughtfully, "that your father suddenly became ill and could no longer work at his blacksmith's shop. Suppose that any money your parents had saved was used up by keeping the household running and seeking medical care. While the shop is still open, your father's hired hand is not able to keep up with all the work and makes very little profit. Are you following me, Mr. Taylor?"

"I'm not sure what you are getting at, sir."

"Under the circumstances that I have described, would you not consider it a reasonable request if your father were to ask you to contribute to the family finances, even if it meant a personal sacrifice on your part?"

"Well, I suppose, if my family needed money to pay for necessary goods, then, yes, I would try to earn some money and give it to my father."

"Think of all of England as your family, and the king as the father who can no longer take care of the family."

"I see what you are saying now," Daniel said. "Massachusetts and the other colonies are the children who need to help support the family."

The teacher raised his eyebrows above his glasses. "I see you understand my point."

"Yes, sir, I understand the comparison. But I believe it is flawed. With all respect, sir, may I explain further?"

"Go right ahead."

"If my father were to ask for my contribution and I were given the opportunity to give it gladly, there would be harmony in the family and all would be well. But suppose my father were to sneak into my bedroom at night and forcibly remove the earnings I have saved without my consent. Justice would suffer greatly, and the family might never be happy again."

"And you believe this is what King George has done—forcibly taken what you have saved, without consent?"

"Yes, sir, I do. Parliament has passed a law forcing us to make payments to the king without having asked us first if we would be willing to do so. This is taxation without representation. And it is a moral wrong."

The teacher reached into his pocket for his watch and examined it.

"Perhaps we can probe this further another day, Mr. Taylor. While such political debate doubtless is better for the mind than what you will engage in once class is dismissed, I am compelled by the statutes of Boston to release you now. Class dismissed."

As Lizzie gathered her books and slate, she glanced over at Joshua. He had wasted no time in seeking out Daniel Taylor, no doubt to hear more of Daniel's opinions about the Stamp Act.

Lizzie did not want to hear more political talk. She had come to believe her father was right. No one wanted a war. The Patriots simply wanted justice, and they would try to achieve it peacefully. In the meantime, though, tension was growing in Boston. Remembering her father's warnings not to walk alone after school, Lizzie quickly collected her light spring shawl and waited on the steps for Joshua.

Spring rains had finally given way to the promise of summer. The day was clear and bright. But Lizzie could not enjoy it. Inside, she was twisted up and confused. If everyone wanted justice and no one wanted a war, why was there so much anger and bitterness in Boston?

When Joshua arrived a few minutes later, he poked her from behind, making her jump.

"Joshua!" She slapped at his hand. "Must you make a joke of absolutely everything?"

"Isn't that Daniel Taylor something?" Joshua said, ignoring Lizzie's irritation. "He really understands the political issues. You should listen to him talk."

"I did listen to him talk, silly."

"No, I don't mean in class. You should have heard the things he said afterward. I believe someday he will be elected to the Massachusetts legislature, maybe even become governor."

"Yes, I suppose he's bright enough." Lizzie did not want to encourage further conversation on politics.

But Joshua had a one-track mind, and on that day the track was politics. "I wonder what his father thinks about all this. He's a blacksmith, after all. He talks to people all day long."

"He talks about shoeing their horses," Lizzie said flatly.

"Ah, yes, but what do they talk about while he is putting the shoes on? He's in a perfect spot to find out what people are thinking."

"Most people just leave the horse and come back when the job is done."

"But not everyone leaves. Some people stay and talk. I've seen them. He could probably write an article for Papa about what people are saying."

Lizzie did not answer. Perhaps her silence would make Joshua find another subject to talk about.

They came around a corner and found themselves at the back of a large group. About twenty people had stopped to watch what was happening across the street, where a bigger crowd was circling a tree.

"What's going on?" Joshua asked, craning his neck to find the focus of attention.

"Over there," someone said. "Under that tree, across the street. Sam Adams is giving a speech."

"Really? Sam Adams?" Joshua asked. Lizzie could hear the excitement in her brother's voice. "What is he talking about?"

"What he always talks about," said a woman. "Freedom. Liberty. How the colonies are in bondage to England and it's time to break free."

"I've never heard him before," Joshua said.

"He's an earful, that's for sure." The woman moved along, having lost interest.

"We should keep going," Lizzie said, nudging Joshua. "Papa will be waiting."

"Just a few minutes," Joshua said, fixing his gaze on Sam Adams across the street. "Look at the way he stands, as if he were the preacher in the finest church in England, instead of standing under a tree that barely has its spring blossoms."

Joshua struck a pose that looked remarkably like Sam Adams. He stood with his feet solidly apart and his hands in the air, elbows up.

"How's this?" he said, grinning at Lizzie.

She smiled. She had to admit his imitation was accurate. "That is really good, Joshua. Now you just need a tattered black coat. Can we go?"

Joshua did not answer. He was busy capturing the gestures of the outdoor speaker. He mimicked the way Sam Adams emphasized his points by thrusting his fists through the air and then pushing his arm straight up over his shoulder with only one finger raised.

"You're quite amusing, young man," said a mother struggling to keep a toddler under control.

"Where did you learn how to do that?" asked someone else.

Lizzie put her head back and rolled her eyes. Joshua had an audience. Now they would be there until suppertime. "Joshua!" she hissed.

But he paid no attention to her. He put his fists on his hips, threw out his chest, and surveyed the crowd, just as Adams was doing across the street.

"You're very good, Joshua," Lizzie said. "Quite convincing. Now can we go?"

"The only problem is that I can't hear him. I don't know

what his voice sounds like."

"I'm sure it's just an ordinary voice."

"No, the voice of a man who gives speeches has a certain quality."

"He's just a man."

"Let's go across the street and get closer."

"Joshua, no, we can't do that!"

"Why on earth not? The man is just giving a simple political speech. This is Boston. People give political speeches all the time." He started to cross the street. Given her father's instructions to stay with Joshua, Lizzie had no choice but to follow. Joshua barely glanced over his shoulder to see if she was there as he worked his way up to the front of the crowd.

"We are not children," Sam Adams was saying when they got close enough to hear his words. "We are mature, educated men of sound minds." He punctuated his sentence with another thrust in the air.

Joshua did the same as he silently echoed Adams's words.

"Joshua, this isn't funny anymore," Lizzie pleaded. "Please, let's go."

Adams continued to talk. "What is one letter from the Massachusetts Assembly to the king of England? Neither New York, nor Pennsylvania, nor Maryland has seen this letter. If the assemblies in these colonies have also sent letters to the king, what does that matter? We have not seen their letters. We may plead one argument while they plead another. In such division there is weakness. The king is right not to be concerned with such disorganization."

Joshua looked at Lizzie. His expression had sobered, and his arms hung motionless at his sides. "You're right; this isn't funny anymore. But we can't go, not yet."

"Joshua, please," Lizzie whispered.

"I think what he says makes a lot of sense, and I want to hear it."

"You know as well as I do that Papa thinks Sam Adams goes too far," Lizzie warned. "He won't like it when he finds out we were late because you wanted to listen to Sam Adams talk under a tree."

"Lizzie, you're only twelve. But I'm nearly fifteen. I have to make up my own mind about these things."

"Suppose, however," Adams said, "that we were to unite in our objections to the king." He seemed to be looking directly at Joshua. "Suppose that instead of receiving a half-dozen different arguments, each of them weak in itself, King George were to receive one forceful document laying out all of the claims of the colonies. In such a circumstance, he would not dare to treat us as ignorant children."

"One letter to the king!" Joshua exclaimed. "Remind me to ask Papa if that has ever been done before."

"It hasn't," Lizzie said flatly.

"How do you know?" Joshua seemed to doubt that a twelve-year-old girl could know much of anything.

Lizzie shrugged. "I'm not as idle as you think. I listen to what is going on. I heard Uncle Blake and Papa talking about the same thing. It would be something called a *congress*."

"A Continental Congress!" Sam Adams said emphatically. "We must take the first step toward giving the colonies the freedom they deserve and the liberty they have earned."

Lizzie pulled as hard as she could on Joshua's elbow. "Joshua, you're keeping me in bondage. Now let's go."

"All right," he finally agreed, "but only because I have some questions for Papa."

CHAPTER 6

The Shooting

The pile of newspapers landed in the back of the cart with a *thwack*. Joshua pushed them to the corner and checked to make sure the string around them was tight.

"How many more?" Lizzie asked. The glare of the summer afternoon sun made her squint.

"Two more trips." Joshua disappeared back into the print shop to tie up more copies of the afternoon paper.

Lizzie inspected the hitch that linked the cart to the horse. Satisfied that Joshua had hitched the cart properly, she turned her attention to the horse.

"Well, Merry," she said, stroking the side of the mare's head, "another round of deliveries. I'm not sure you really need Joshua and me. You've been doing this so long that you know exactly where to go."

Merry neighed softly and moved her head about, nuzzling Lizzie's hand.

Lizzie laughed. "You're looking for sugar, aren't you, girl? I'm sorry, but sugar is hard to come by these days. Mama says sugar is getting too expensive for people, much less for a horse. I do have an apple."

Lizzie produced the fruit, and Merry accepted it enthusiastically.

Joshua appeared with another stack of newspapers. He scowled at Lizzie.

"I don't think playing with the horse counts as part of helping with the route," he said sternly.

Lizzie made a face. "I'm making sure Merry is ready."

"Merry has been doing this since we were babies. Believe me, she's ready."

"Let me drive today," Lizzie said.

"Aw, Lizzie!"

"Come on, Joshua. Merry is gentle. She knows the route. Nothing will happen."

"I could do this without you, you know," Joshua said.

"And I could do it without you. But Papa said to stay together."

Joshua surrendered. "Turn the cart around while I get the last stack."

Gleefully, Lizzie hiked up her skirts and climbed into the seat of the carriage. Twelve was a strange age, she had decided. She was old enough to know how adults behaved, and her parents expected her to behave like an adult. Yet she was young enough to enjoy the simple pleasure of riding in a cart and making the horse go where she wanted it to go. This was the first summer that Papa had let her drive the cart for more than a few yards, and she had been practicing for weeks. The sense of responsibility made her feel even more grown-up. She maneuvered the cart around so that she was facing the street and waited. A moment later, Joshua appeared with the last stack of papers. He threw it into the cart, then climbed in the back and sat on top of the stack.

"Ready?" Lizzie asked brightly.

"I'm never ready when you're driving," Joshua muttered.

Lizzie ignored him and nudged Merry with the reins. The old mare needed little encouragement to begin her trot down the main streets of Boston. They would stop periodically to drop papers off for agents to sell or sometimes stand on a corner and sell papers themselves.

"Good day, Mr. Kearney," Joshua said as he tossed a small pile off the cart.

"G'day to ye both," Mr. Kearney answered. "And how be the wee ones at home?"

Lizzie smiled. "Olivia and Emmett are just fine. Thank you for asking."

They trotted on.

"I'm going to give Uncle Philip a double stack today," Joshua said. "He told Papa that more and more people who come by the clinic want to read the paper."

Lizzie narrowed her eyes and looked straight ahead. "Joshua?" she said softly.

"Did you hear what I said about Uncle Philip?" Joshua persisted.

"Yes, he's the next stop. But, Joshua, look." Lizzie pulled on the reins slightly, and Merry broke her rhythm and stopped.

Joshua clamored over the piles of newspapers to look out the front of the cart. Two British soldiers stood poised

LIZZIE AND THE REDCOAT

on the street corner, squaring off against a dozen or more young colonists.

"What's going on, Joshua?" Lizzie's stomach churned.

Joshua shook his head. "I can't tell from here. Get closer."

"I don't think we should."

"Lizzie," Joshua said impatiently, "you said you wanted to drive. Now drive!"

Reluctantly, she got Merry started again, and they drew up closer to the encounter.

"Why don't you redcoats leave us alone and go home?" a man shouted.

"We did not come to stir up trouble," one of the soldiers said. "We simply want to pass this way to go to the docks."

"Why do you need to go to the docks?" another voice challenged.

Lizzie nudged Joshua. "Isn't that Daniel Taylor?"

Joshua nodded silently.

"With all due respect, we have jobs at the docks, and we are late already. Please let us pass."

"You don't need to work at the docks!" Daniel Taylor shouted. "You already have a job. The king pays you to do his bidding."

"The pay is not enough, and if you people in the colonies would recognize that, we would have no quarrel between us." The British soldier was clearly losing his patience.

"Let's all take pity on the redcoats," Daniel said in an exaggerated tone of voice. "They have only one set of clothes, after all." Daniel turned to his friends for encouragement, and they began shouting at the soldiers.

"Go home to England to get a real job!"

"If you leave us alone, we'll leave you alone!"

"Go home to your precious king and tell him your troubles. We don't want to hear them."

The soldiers glanced at each other, then started to force their way through the roadblock the young men had set up.

"Don't you shove me!" one of the young men shouted. And then he swung his fist at the nearest soldier.

"Joshua!" Lizzie cried. "Do something!"

"I'll try to talk to Daniel and get him to call off his friends." Joshua looked sternly at Lizzie. "You stay right here. Do you hear me? Don't move."

Lizzie nodded. She was too frightened to move. Where did he think she would go?

Joshua jumped down from the cart and dashed toward the group on the corner. He pushed past several young men until he found Daniel Taylor.

"Daniel," Joshua started. "Daniel, please, what are you doing?"

"This is none of your business, Joshua," Daniel said.

"I just don't want anyone to get hurt," Joshua said. "Please, tell your friends to go home. There is no need for a fight."

"Is that what you think?" one of the other young men said. "If you get in our way, that means you are siding with the redcoats."

"I'm not siding with anyone!" Joshua exclaimed. "I just don't think there is any need for a fight."

The man pushed his fist up under Joshua's chin.

Lizzie gasped, and as she did so, she let go of the reins. Merry started moving again.

"No, Merry, no!" Lizzie cried, scrambling to pick up the reins.

The old mare paid no attention to Lizzie's pleas. She continued her trot and walked right past the corner where Joshua stood. Desperately, Lizzie looked back over her shoulder at the fracas on the corner. Joshua ducked just in time to avoid being punched in the eye.

"Joshua!" Lizzie screamed. "Merry, stop! Stop!" Leaning as far forward out of her seat as she dared, she grasped for the loose reins. Finally, she had hold of them again. Immediately, she pulled Merry to a stop, jumped down, and tied the reins around a post. Then she scrambled back to the corner where she had left Joshua.

To her surprise and relief, Uncle Philip had just come out of his clinic and was trying to break up the fight. Fists and foul names were flying everywhere. Lizzie could hardly keep track of which arms belonged to which bodies.

"Joshua!" she called out as she ran toward him.

Uncle Philip heard her scream and turned toward her. Just at that moment, one of the strongest young men in the bunch swung a board. The side of Uncle Philip's face and the board collided. When she heard the *crack*, Lizzie could not tell if it was the board or Uncle Philip's skull that had broken.

He slumped to the ground.

"Uncle Philip!" she screamed. "Joshua, help him!"

"Lizzie, stay out of this!" Somehow Joshua's voice rose to the top of the chaos. But Lizzie could not keep out. She ran toward her uncle. Just as she reached him, Uncle Philip sat up groggily. He held his head in his hands.

"Uncle Philip, are you all right?" Lizzie knelt beside him and gently touched his face.

Uncle Philip groaned. "I'm all right, Lizzie. You should do what Joshua says and get away."

"I can't leave you here like this."

"I'm all right, Lizzie. You must be careful for your own safety."

Helping Uncle Philip to his feet, Lizzie gasped again. One of Daniel Taylor's friends wielded a gun. Uncle Philip gripped Lizzie's shoulders and prevented her from moving.

"Daniel, stop this madness," Joshua pleaded. "Tell him to put the gun away."

"A man with a gun does what he pleases." The man spoke before Daniel could say anything.

"Just let the soldiers pass," Joshua said.

The man pivoted and pointed the gun at Joshua. Lizzie stifled a scream.

"Nobody will get hurt who doesn't deserve to get hurt," the man said. "You decide which side you're on, once and for all."

Lizzie held her breath, not knowing what Joshua would do or say. He said nothing. He did nothing.

In the scuffle that came next, it was hard to tell who did what. All Lizzie knew was that the man with the musket was pounced on by several of his cohorts. Apparently others in the gang had the good sense to know that their friend should not be trusted with a loaded musket. Lizzie saw the tip of the muzzle arching upward when it went off.

"Joshua!" But it was not Joshua who dropped to the cobblestone. It was one of the British soldiers, shot through the shoulder.

Uncle Philip released Lizzie and rushed past her to the fallen soldier. "Let me help," he called out. "I'm a doctor."

"We know who you are," sneered one of the men. "We heard the tailor was fitting you for a redcoat all your own."

Uncle Philip put his ear to the soldier's chest. "This man is badly wounded, but he's alive. Let me help him."

"Leave him be," said the man who had fired the musket. "Nature will finish my interrupted work."

"Have you gone mad?" said one of the others. "Take your musket and get out of here before the authorities arrive." Two others scurried away, taking with them the man who had shot the soldier.

"Joshua! Lizzie! Help me." Putting his hand behind the soldier's back, Uncle Philip propped up the wounded redcoat. The soldier's head rolled from side to side like a loose ball.

"Daniel," Joshua pleaded, "stop this insanity."

Daniel's face had gone white. He put his hands up. "It is out of my hands now. You decide for yourself what you are going to do."

Where she found the courage, Lizzie did not know. But she knew that she had to respond to her uncle's pleas for help. She squatted in the street with Uncle Philip and tried to lift the unconscious soldier to his feet. Blood flowed from his wound onto her dress and hands.

"We have to get him to the clinic," Uncle Philip said, "away from these brutes."

"They'll never let us in," Lizzie said.

"Only a redcoat would help another redcoat!" a voice shouted.

"You had better think carefully about your next step, Wallace."

"Ignore them, Lizzie," Uncle Philip said. "Start walking. Look straight at the clinic door, nothing else."

Lizzie nodded, squelching the sob that welled up in her throat.

"Clear the way!" Joshua shouted. He started pushing his way through the gang.

Uncle Philip grunted. "I know he's heavy, Lizzie, but go as quickly as you can."

A spray of stones splattered Lizzie's face.

"Girls can be redcoats, too, you know."

The angry words stung almost as much as the stones themselves.

"The clinic door, Lizzie," came Uncle Philip's steady voice. "Nothing else."

CHAPTER 7

The Wounded Soldier

Lizzie lurched across the threshold, catching herself just in time to keep from stumbling. Her thin shoulders bore the weight of the unconscious soldier. His lanky form was draped haphazardly between Lizzie and Uncle Philip. Her knees nearly buckled with every step, and her stomach churned violently.

Uncle Philip tugged her through the doorway and pointed at a cot along one wall. The mob was at their heels, screaming disapproval.

"Lobsterback!"

"Traitor!"

"Even doctors have to pay taxes!"

Lizzie craned her neck for a glance at the men outside. Instead, she saw the back of Joshua's head as he crashed the wooden door shut behind them.

"Secure the latch!" Uncle Philip shouted. "And get away from the window. Now!"

Joshua obediently pulled down the latch and stepped toward the center of the room, but he turned his head to look out the window.

"We need your help, Joshua," Uncle Philip said sharply. "Pay attention in here, please."

"What do you want us to do?" Lizzie asked, certain that she could bear the soldier's weight no longer.

"Joshua, help me lay him on the cot," Uncle Philip directed, taking the weight of the soldier from Lizzie. "Lizzie, get a bucket of water. You'll find some clean rags in the cupboard."

Lizzie surrendered her responsibility for the soldier to Joshua and turned toward the cupboards on the facing wall. Her lungs burst with the realization that she had not taken a deep breath in a long while. She gulped some new air and forced herself to move toward the cupboard. Uncle Philip's voice sounded distant, somewhere beyond the pounding of her own heart. Bleary with sweat and tears she had not known she was shedding, Lizzie's eyes refused to focus. She wiped her eyes with the back of her grimy hands and only then saw that her sleeve was drenched with the soldier's blood.

"Quickly, Lizzie," Uncle Philip urged as he straightened the soldier's form on the cot.

Lizzie blinked her eyes into focus, yanked open the cupboard door, and grabbed an armful of clean rags. The water barrel stood in the corner. She nervously filled a bucket and carried it to Uncle Philip.

"Good." Uncle Philip had unfastened the red jacket, the symbol hated by so many Bostonians, and was trying to pull the man's shirt away from his chest. Blood matted the white cotton cloth, causing the cloth to stick to the soldier's skin. "Joshua, stoke the fire. I don't want him to get cold."

Joshua started to protest. "But it's warm in—"

"Do as I say!" Uncle Philip cut him off, and Joshua picked up the iron to stir up the coals Uncle Philip always kept ready for service. "There is wood in the back room. Get what you need."

Joshua scurried into action, knowing better than to argue further.

"We'll have to expose the wound, Lizzie. I'll need a knife. There is one on the sideboard. We'll have to cut through his shirt and jacket to get at the wound in his shoulder."

Lizzie handed her uncle the knife and grimaced as he first slit the cloth of the man's jacket, then the shirt. Gently he pried the blood-soaked garment away from the skin. Lizzie clenched her stomach as she watched Uncle Philip work. The hole in the soldier's shoulder gaped up at her, still spurting dark purple liquid. Her hand moved to her mouth to stifle a scream.

"Stay with me, Lizzie," Uncle Philip said, his voice more gentle than before. "I need your help."

She swallowed hard and took a deep breath. "What do you need?" She grasped the back of a chair to keep from quaking. Her voice sounded braver than she felt.

"A wet cloth. Lots of water."

Lizzie dipped a rag in the bucket and handed it, still dripping, to Uncle Philip. In a few seconds, Uncle Philip had the area cleansed. Still the blood came.

"Should I get Aunt Johanna?" Lizzie asked hopefully. She knew her aunt was experienced at assisting Uncle

Philip in emergency situations, as well as in the routine care of patients.

"There's no time. He's bleeding too much. Besides, you would never get out the door. Lizzie, you can do this. I know you can."

"I'm trying, Uncle Philip. It's just. . .the blood."

"You're doing fine. Just follow my instructions."

Lizzie nodded.

"Put your hand here," Uncle Philip said, pointing to the wound. He laid a fresh cloth over it and guided Lizzie's hand. "Now press down, and keep pressure on the wound."

A clatter of wood behind her made Lizzie jump.

"Keep pressing," came Uncle Philip's steady voice.

Lizzie threw a frightened glance toward the window. But the sound had come from Joshua returning from the back room with an armload of wood.

"How is he?" Joshua asked, arranging three logs on the fire and stirring up the coals once again. The dry wood immediately began to crackle. Bright flames spurted upward and threw shadows on the walls. Lizzie pressed harder.

Uncle Philip sighed. "He'll be all right if we can get the bleeding to stop. But he's still unconscious."

"Why?"

"Probably from the pain. We have to keep him warm." Uncle Philip unfolded a wool blanket on the end of the cot and spread it over the soldier's legs.

Joshua drew closer and studied the patient's face. Knotted light brown hair framed his pale face. "He's so young," Joshua said softly, thoughtfully.

"Just a boy," Uncle Philip agreed. "Hardly more than sixteen, I'd say."

"Two years older than I am," Joshua murmured, his eyes wide with the realization of his coming manhood.

"Did you see his boots?" Lizzie asked. "I could see newspaper wrapped around his feet showing right through the bottom of one of them, and the other is not much better. He probably hasn't been to the cobbler in two years."

"Keep pressing, Lizzie," Uncle Philip said as he felt for the young man's pulse. "A lot of the British soldiers are in the same condition. That's part of why Parliament has ordered the stamp tax—to provide for the soldiers on duty in the colonies."

"But, Uncle Philip," Joshua started, "there must be another way. Taxing us when we have no part in Parliament's decisions simply is not fair."

"But we do receive protection from the Crown."

"Why can't we pay the soldiers ourselves, like we always have?" Joshua persisted in his argument.

Uncle Philip shook his head. "There are no easy answers. But sending boys like this—or you—into dangerous situations is not fair, either."

Joshua had no response. He knew his uncle was right.

Lizzie tried to imagine Joshua across the ocean, thousands of miles away from his home, following orders whether he agreed with them or not. Then she imagined how their parents would feel—how the soldier's parents must be feeling right at that moment—not knowing the fate of their son.

Outside, the mob throbbed against the clinic walls. Lizzie could hear their rocks striking the door. Uncle Philip casually glanced out the window, but Lizzie saw his concern. Joshua, too, studied his uncle's expression. Lizzie reached for a fresh rag and eyed her brother.

"Do you wish you were out there with them, Joshua?"

Joshua's eyes met hers briefly and then shifted away. "Don't be foolish."

"This could have been you!" Lizzie cried. "You could be lying in the street with no one to take care of you. Boston is dangerous enough these days. You're getting mixed up with Sam Adams, and that will only make things worse."

"You worry too much," Joshua replied.

Lizzie glared at him.

Uncle Philip checked on the wound. Lizzie looked down at her hands, covered in blood, and remembered the injury her uncle had taken in the fracas. "Uncle Philip, is your head all right?"

He touched his forehead, which was swollen and blue. "I will confess that I have a blinding headache, but I am certain it will subside in a few minutes."

"I felt so helpless when I saw that board aimed at your head. I don't know what I would have done if you had been hurt badly."

Uncle Philip smiled at her. "You would have done what

you are doing now—taking care of the wounded."

Lizzie shook her head. "No, I wouldn't have known what to do without your help."

"You're doing a wonderful job, Lizzie."

His words made her calmer. Then she saw a face in the window, and her heart lurched. "Won't they ever stop?" she cried.

"Philip Wallace!" came the voice from outside, muffled by the glass. "You'll have to answer for giving refuge to a lobsterback." A spray of pebbles tinkled against the pane.

"Pay them no mind, Lizzie," her uncle said, wiping his own face with a cool cloth.

"But they might break the door down."

Philip shook his head. "If they were going to do that, they would have done it by now." He stepped over to the window. "Most of them have dispersed. The ones who are left are just agitating to make a name for themselves."

"The Sons of Liberty, no doubt!" Lizzie said scornfully.

"The Sons of Liberty are not agitators," Joshua said in defense of the friendships he had formed during the summer months. "They want to do what's best for the colonies."

"Rioting in the streets is good for the colonies?" Lizzie gave voice to her skepticism.

"Now stay calm, you two," Uncle Philip warned. "We don't need a civil war in the family as well as out in the streets."

A moan brought them all back to the reason they were in the clinic together. The soldier moved his head stiffly from side to side, and his eyes fluttered open.

Uncle Philip put a hand on Lizzie's shoulder. "I think the bleeding has stopped." He tried to nudge her away, but she was frozen in her spot. Her green eyes locked onto the gaze of the clear gray eyes of the soldier, and she saw in him the same fear that was in her own heart.

"It's all right, son," Uncle Philip said, gently prying Lizzie's hand off the soldier's chest. "I'm a doctor. I want to help you."

The young man moaned once again.

"I'm sure you are in a great deal of pain," Uncle Philip said, "and I will do what I can to make you comfortable. You'll have to stay for a few days until your wound is sufficiently healed."

The soldier's eyes followed Uncle Philip's movements as he examined him more fully.

"I'll arrange everything with your captain," Uncle Philip said. "Do you think you could manage to sit up a bit so we can take off your shirt and coat?"

The young man slowly turned his head toward his wound and spoke for the first time. "You cut my coat."

"We had to," Uncle Philip said calmly. "It was the only way to get to the wound and stop the bleeding."

"You cut my coat," the soldier repeated, his voice cracking. "It's my only coat."

"I'm sorry about that, truly I am, but surely you can understand the need."

The soldier turned his eyes away. "You cut my coat," he

said again, softly, with defeat in his voice.

"Lizzie," Uncle Philip said quietly, motioning for her to help strip off the mutilated clothing. Gently, he supported the young man from the back, while Lizzie slowly worked the shirt and jacket off. She saw the soldier's thin chest and the bumps his ribs made. *When did he last have a good meal?* she wondered. Even in the midst of a boycott, her family managed to eat. None of them were as thin as this soldier.

Joshua moved restlessly back and forth across the room, stirring the fire and checking the window. Uncle Philip and Lizzie did not speak as they finished cleaning the grime off the soldier and bandaging his wound. The soldier grimaced in pain, but he did not moan again. When the job was done, he breathed heavily and fell asleep once more.

Lizzie joined Joshua at the window. Only two boys remained outside, and they were simply amusing themselves kicking rocks. Joshua turned once again toward the soldier.

"He's so young," Joshua said. "So young."

CHAPTER 8

Aunt Johanna's Visit

Lizzie jumped out of her chair. Her book slid down the folds of her skirts to the floor. Sudden pounding on the front door had broken into her afternoon reading on a hot August day. She had been looking for an excuse to put aside the reading her mother had assigned her, but she had hoped for a more pleasant interruption.

"Coming!" she called out. She clutched her skirts and ran as quickly as she could across the front room toward the door.

At the same time, she heard her mother's footsteps rushing from the kitchen and Joshua thundering down the stairs. The pounding continued—this time even more insistently. The three of them converged on the front door, competing to be the one to pull it open and reveal the source of the ruckus.

"Aunt Johanna!" Lizzie said, shocked when the door was finally open.

"Johanna, get inside this instant," Constance Murray grabbed her sister-in-law by the forearm and pulled her into the house. Before closing the door again, she scanned the street outside the house. Looking over her mother's shoulder, Lizzie could see nothing.

With Aunt Johanna was young Charity, who looked

confused but secure in her mother's arms. She smiled at Lizzie and curled her fingers in a wave.

"Aunt Johanna, what's happened?" Lizzie questioned. "You look as white as a ghost."

Before answering, Aunt Johanna set her young daughter down securely on the floor and straightened her dress. "Charity, run upstairs and look for Emmett, please. It's playtime."

"Playtime!" squealed Charity. And before anyone said another word, she was gone.

Aunt Johanna let out a heavy sigh and smoothed her frazzled hair.

"Come in the kitchen, Johanna, and I'll fix you some tea," Mama said. She nodded at her daughter. "Lizzie, get the cups out."

"Yes, Mama." Lizzie obeyed her mother with her hands, but her ears, eyes, and mind were all fixed on her aunt.

Mama stoked the fire under the pot to boil the water. Aunt Johanna sank into a chair. Joshua glanced out the window.

"Now tell us what happened," Mama said.

"I'm so sorry to barge in on you in such a rude manner," Aunt Johanna said. "I suddenly felt that I must get off the street, and yours was the nearest house of someone I could trust."

"But what happened?" Joshua pressed his aunt.

"Yes, Aunt Johanna," Lizzie said. "Something must have happened to make you feel that way."

"I'm almost embarrassed to say that nothing exactly happened. At least not yet. It's just that the street gangs make me so nervous. I especially hate to go out when I have Charity with me, but Philip was too busy at the clinic to watch her, and I couldn't avoid going out any longer."

Joshua moved to the window and peered outside. "Street gangs, you say?"

"Yes. This time it was Douglas Taylor's son and his rowdies."

"Daniel?"

"Yes, that's his name." Aunt Johanna gratefully accepted the tea that Mama poured.

"Are they out there now?" Joshua asked.

"They were a few minutes ago. Down the street a bit. They had no clear purpose that I could see."

Scenes from her own encounter with Daniel Taylor's gang flashed through Lizzie's mind. "You did the right thing to come here," she said, "especially when you had Charity with you."

"You mustn't take any chances," Mama said as she offered her sister-in-law some precious sugar for her tea.

"This is all the fault of Sam Adams!" Aunt Johanna exclaimed.

Joshua wheeled around. "What do you mean? Sam Adams is not part of that gang."

"No, but he has his own gang, and their presence in Boston grows stronger every day. Other people start gangs to be like him."

"Daniel and his friends just like to push people around. Sam Adams is trying to get something done."

"Their activities look very much alike to me," Aunt Johanna insisted.

Joshua was not satisfied. "I've never heard Sam say anything about terrorizing women and children in the street."

Aunt Johanna sipped the tea. "He doesn't have to say that in so many words. If he would stop standing under that silly Liberty Tree giving speeches, Boston might settle down."

Joshua looked away and said nothing.

Mama lowered herself into a chair next to Aunt Johanna. "I heard that the Shreves were forced to house two British soldiers against their will."

"Have you seen those soldiers, Constance?" Aunt Johanna asked. "They are nothing but boys who are too far from home. If it were Joshua, you would be glad to have someone take him in and give him a decent meal."

"But the Shreves have five children of their own, and they can hardly keep them fed as it is. Now they have two more full-grown men to feed. I can't imagine how they are going to do it—especially since Levi Shreve is one of the most outspoken Patriots in Boston."

"Oh, Mama, you haven't heard, have you?" Lizzie said. Instantly she wished she could take back her words.

"Haven't heard what, Lizzie?"

Lizzie's fingers twisted around the ties of her apron. "The Shreves don't have to house the soldiers anymore. One of the gangs—"

"Don't tell me!" Mama exclaimed. "One of those crazy gangs broke into the Shreve house and threw the furniture around."

Lizzie nodded mutely. "There isn't much left. I saw Mr.

Shreve's daughter Alyce outside the print shop yesterday. She won't be able to come back to school. They have to move away."

"But the house, the furniture—none of that belongs to the British soldiers. What is the point in destroying personal property needlessly?"

Aunt Johanna shook her head. "Do you see what I mean now?"

"You don't know for sure that Sam Adams is behind those activities," Joshua said. "Sam is trying to unite the colonies in an organized protest against Parliament. That's the only reason he goes around town talking."

"Sam Adams is doing far more than talking," Aunt Johanna said. "Talking doesn't hurt people. But families are being destroyed. People are losing homes that they have worked hard for—homes their parents built. I am on my knees every night asking God to bring an end to this madness."

Lizzie needed to keep herself busy while she sorted out what she was hearing. She stood up abruptly and started straightening the chairs around the table. Aunt Johanna had always been the person Lizzie could turn to when she was most confused. But right now, Aunt Johanna sounded just as confused as Lizzie was herself.

"I'm going to check on the children," Mama said.

"I'll just take a look down the street," Joshua said casually.

Aunt Johanna and Lizzie were alone. Lizzie's mind burst with questions she wanted to ask. She hardly knew where to begin.

"Aunt Johanna?" Lizzie stopped her fidgeting and stood with her hands on the back of a chair.

"Yes, Lizzie, what is it?"

"Do you think Sam Adams is in charge of Boston?"

Aunt Johanna smiled and sighed. "You remember what we talked about at Christmas, don't you?"

Lizzie nodded. "But you seem different now." She dropped into the chair beside her aunt. "Back then you seemed to know that nothing bad was really going to happen because God was in control. But now. . .now you seem as angry as everyone else in Boston."

"You may be right, Lizzie. These last eight months have been such a strain. Why, look at what happened to you and Joshua only a few days ago."

"And Uncle Philip."

"I thank God you were not hurt and that Philip suffered only a bad headache. But I can't promise you that no one in our family is ever going to be hurt. So, yes, sometimes I am frightened and angry." She laughed. "I guess I must sound quite ridiculous going on about Sam Adams, as if he were mightier than God Himself. No, Lizzie, I do not think Sam Adams is in charge of Boston. God is still in charge."

"Then why is everyone angry all the time?"

Aunt Johanna sighed slowly. "That is a question I cannot answer. But God will work this out. I am sure of that."

Mama reappeared in the kitchen doorway. "Lizzie," she said, "perhaps you could take the children out in the garden for a little while. It's such a beautiful day. I'm sure if you stayed in the back, near the house, you would be quite safe."

Lizzie looked from her mother to Aunt Johanna. Her aunt nodded. "Go on, Lizzie. I would like it if Charity could play in the fresh air."

"Yes, ma'am," Lizzie said, and stood up. She pushed her chair in neatly under the table.

At moments like this, she hated being twelve. Mama and Aunt Johanna were going to have a discussion that would no doubt be more interesting than playing with three small children. But she would not be allowed even to overhear it from the next room.

Olivia, Emmett, and Charity charged past her and out the back door into the yard. Lizzie reluctantly followed. Outside, she sat on a tree stump and surveyed her surroundings.

The yard was quite pleasant, actually. The children could play in a large square of grass, hidden from the street. And beyond the play yard were the flower gardens. Her mother had worked hard all summer to make the flowers grow, and they were in full bloom. Their colors melted from one shade into another and cascaded across the property. Behind the flower gardens was the vegetable patch. Soon it would be time to pick the beans and squash and store them for the winter. Lizzie had been helping with that process for as long as she could remember. At the back of the lot, the ground sloped up, forming a stubby hill for winter sledding.

Lizzie shook her head. How could she be thinking about flowers and vegetables, knowing that her mother and her aunt were sitting in the kitchen discussing the hazards of life in Boston? Her uncle was still tending a wounded British soldier and being criticized because of his decision to care for the man. Her father was under pressure to use his newspaper and printing press in a revolt against the Stamp Act. Yet she was longing for fresh vegetables and white, smooth snow.

She looked up at the frolicking children, who were chasing each other around the enclosed yard. Olivia had recently graduated out of the clothes of toddlers and into the dresses of older girls and women. But she was unconcerned with ladylike behavior at that moment. She tackled Emmett, and they tumbled to the ground, squealing.

Lizzie sincerely hoped that all the children thought about was flowers and vegetables and when they would next be able to play together. Olivia was boisterous, and it was not always easy to tell what she was feeling. Emmett had a sensitive spirit; he probably understood more than he talked about. Charity was full of common sense. If she were a few years older, she would no doubt have her own opinions about how to solve Boston's problems in the way that made the most sense.

"Where is Joshua going?" Emmett's fragile voice broke into Lizzie's musings.

"What do you mean?"

Emmett pointed. Joshua was closing the door carefully behind him, making sure it would not slam. He carried a small leather pack. Lizzie jumped off her stump.

"Joshua?" she said loudly.

He put a finger to his lips to hush her. She gathered up

her skirts and ran over to him before he could get away.

"Where are you going?" she said in a half whisper.

"It's better if you don't know."

"That's ridiculous, Joshua." She stamped her foot. "Tell me where you are going."

"Lizzie, this is not your business."

"You're my brother. Of course it is my business."

Joshua looked toward the kitchen window. They could see their aunt and mother still engrossed in conversation.

"Aunt Johanna is wrong," Joshua said. "Sam Adams is not responsible for what happened to us the other day."

"Oh, Joshua, she was just letting out her frustration. She was frightened. Can you blame her?"

"No. I don't blame her for being frightened. But she's wrong about Sam Adams."

"Where are you going?" Lizzie asked again.

Joshua shook his head. He was not going to tell her.

"Why are you taking your pack?" Lizzie persisted.

Again, Joshua only shook his head.

"Something is happening tonight, isn't it, Joshua?" Lizzie said. "Aunt Johanna is frightened for a good reason, isn't she?"

"Lizzie, please, I'm not going to say anything more. Please let me be!" He turned to go.

"Joshua?" Lizzie said softly.

With a groan of frustration, Joshua turned to face her again.

"Take care of yourself."

CHAPTER 9

What Joshua Saw

Punching her pillow, Lizzie wondered what time it was—again. Then she answered her own question. It was ten minutes later than the last time she had punched her pillow and wondered what time it was. Her bedding was a tangled mess. Across the room, Olivia slept serenely. Lizzie could hardly believe that anyone, even an exhausted child, could sleep through the night that had just passed. Lizzie herself had not slept a minute all night.

When Joshua had not arrived for supper, her mother and father had turned their attention to Lizzie. They were convinced that she would know where to find him. Since Lizzie and Joshua had been instructed to stay together when they were walking around town, her parents reasoned that she had been everywhere that Joshua had been in recent days. Lizzie reminded them that although she had been forbidden to go out alone, Joshua was still free to come and go as he pleased. Surely he had had many opportunities for conversations or activities that Lizzie knew nothing about.

Mama had burned the supper, and no one ate much. The silence at the table was broken only by Mama's occasional coaxing to get Olivia and Emmett to eat a few bites.

Lizzie had cleared the table and washed the dishes without being asked. Hardly noticing her efforts, her parents went out looking for Joshua. By then he had been missing for several hours. Lizzie tucked Olivia and Emmett into bed—over their protests about the absence of their parents—and sat alone in the front room. She tried to focus her thoughts on the usual sounds of a summer evening: crickets in the grass, horses clip-clopping on the cobblestone, boys playing with sticks and rocks in front of the house next door. But she did not hear those sounds. Carriages rumbled past the house, one after the other. Their tumult drowned out the crickets' song, and the boys were shouting patriotic slogans instead of keeping score on their game.

Something was going on in the street that night. Every few minutes, Lizzie got out of her chair to part the drapes and peek outside. People ought to be finishing supper and settling in for the night. Why were so many people running around the streets? Even if she could muster the courage to investigate, she dared not leave Olivia and Emmett alone in the house to go find out.

And what did Joshua know about all this? For surely he had known before this all began. His steadfast refusal that afternoon to tell her where he was going had been the beginning of her suspicion.

When the light grew dim, Lizzie did not bother to light a lamp. She simply sat wondering where Joshua was and what he was doing, and worrying about what her parents might find. As best she could, she prayed that Mama and Papa would find Joshua and bring him home safely. She wanted to believe, as Aunt Johanna did, that they were all in God's hands, whether what happened was good or bad. Lizzie sat in the dark, listening to her heart pound and wondering if she could ever believe that.

Mama and Papa came home at last. They were alone. They had covered a dozen square miles in their search, and Joshua was nowhere to be found. Once again they questioned Lizzie, and once again she could tell them nothing.

"What is happening out there?" she asked them. "Why are so many people moving about the streets at such a late hour?"

Mama and Papa looked at each other. Mama put her hands to her temples and closed her eyes. Papa put one arm around his wife's shoulders and met his daughter's questioning face.

"We're not sure what is happening, Lizzie. The streets are in chaos. We were concerned only with finding Joshua. But everywhere we went, we heard people talking about Sam Adams."

"Joshua is with Sam Adams, isn't he?"

Papa nodded. "That's what we think. We couldn't find him. We'll pray he comes home safely in the morning when all this is over."

"But what if he doesn't?" Lizzie cried.

"We'll pray that he will."

Mama had ordered Lizzie to bed at eleven o'clock. She had heard the town clock strike every hour since then.

SISTERS IN TIME

Twice she had gotten up to check on Emmett in the room next door. Both times she had seen that her parents still had a lamp burning downstairs. They did not come upstairs all night. Between concern for Joshua and the commotion in the street, sleep was impossible for Lizzie and her parents.

At long last, light filtered through the curtains of Lizzie's bedroom. She judged the time to be about five o'clock in the morning, still too early to get out of bed without being sent back to her room as soon as her mother saw her.

Then the front door creaked open. Lizzie heard the muffled voices of her parents greeting Joshua with both relief and anger. When they moved through the hall and into the kitchen, she could not hear anything. She lay still and waited, wondering if they would send Joshua straight up to his room. Finally, she could stand it no longer. Lizzie got out of bed, wrapped a light shawl around her shoulders, and crept down the stairs.

Downstairs, she pressed herself against the wall of the dining room so she could see Joshua through the doorway without being seen by her parents. He sat in a chair pulled back from the kitchen table. He was covered in soot, his breeches were torn, and he was so tired he could hardly hold his head up. But Lizzie barely noticed all that. What she saw was the fire in his eyes, the excitement, the passion. Wherever he had been, whatever he had done, he had been changed by the experience.

"You can come in, Lizzie," her mother said.

Lizzie stepped into full view. "I'm sorry, Mama. I

couldn't sleep. I've been worried all night."

"I know. Come and have some tea."

Lizzie sat across from Joshua and let her mother set a teacup in front of her.

"Joshua," Papa began, "you have to know we disapprove of these street riots. I cannot imagine what possessed your mind to think you should be involved in one."

"Please let me explain, Papa," Joshua said. "Let me tell you what happened."

Mama pressed her lips together and then said, "All right, tell us what you saw."

"It's true that I knew something was going to happen," Joshua said, "but I didn't know when. I had heard rumors for several days. Then, when Aunt Johanna said she had seen Daniel Taylor and his gang just down the street, I knew that the day had come."

"The day for what?" Mama asked. "Street riots have been common in Boston since the Stamp Act was announced. Why was this day different?"

Joshua turned to his father. "Papa, did you see the effigies hanging from the Liberty Tree yesterday?"

"Effigies?" Lizzie asked. "What are effigies?"

"Effigies are like full-sized puppets," Papa explained. "Dummies of real people."

"Right," Joshua said. "Did you see them?"

"Yes, I did. One looked like Andrew Oliver, who is supposed to distribute the stamps."

"And the other was Lord Bute, the king's adviser," Joshua

explained. "Sam Adams has been talking about those effigies for a while now. But I didn't see them until I went out in the afternoon."

"They burned them, didn't they?" Mama said. "I saw the smoke last night when we were looking for you."

"Do you approve of this, Joshua?" Papa asked.

"Papa, I don't think burning a bunch of paper made up to look like a person hurts anyone. I don't think the stamp tax is a fair one, and the people have a right to protest." He sighed and looked down at his hands. "If only it had stopped there."

"But it didn't, did it?" Papa said sharply. "It never does."

"Daniel was in the middle of it, Papa, suggesting all sorts of terrible things—tearing up people's houses, burning ships, things like that. I thought if I could talk to him, make him see that he was accomplishing nothing, perhaps he would go home and leave well enough alone for the night."

"And did he?" Lizzie asked.

Joshua nodded. "Yes, after they burned the effigies, he told his boys to go home. But they were just a bunch of boys, Papa! There were so many men out there—real men—that it hardly mattered that Daniel went home."

"We heard the racket for half the night, Joshua," Mama said, "but you might as well tell us everything that happened."

"They went to Andrew Oliver's private dock in the harbor."

"To the stamp building?" Papa asked.

Joshua nodded. "They tore it apart, board by board. It

wasn't even finished being built yet, but they tore it down. Just because it was supposed to store the stamps. I stood there feeling completely helpless! I don't agree with the Stamp Act any more than any of the other people down there, but it was a mob. They tore down a building. I couldn't get anyone to listen to me. Tearing down a building is not going to stop the stamps from coming. They'll build another building or rent one from a Loyalist."

Papa put his hand on his son's shoulder. Joshua put his elbows on the table and lowered his head into his hands.

"After that," he continued, "they went to Oliver's house and started tearing up his garden. A lot of the men wanted to break into the house, but Lieutenant Governor Hutchinson arrived with the sheriff, and that slowed things down a bit. Some of the people went home then. But a lot of others just stood there yelling and making threats. Finally Oliver came out."

"He came out into that mob?" Lizzie could not believe what she heard.

"Well, not right out into the mob. There's a balcony on his house. He stood on the balcony and promised to resign as stamp distributor."

Mama sighed. "That won't stop anything, either. The authorities in England will appoint another stamp distributor."

"Yes," said Lizzie, "somebody like Ezra Byles, who doesn't care what anyone thinks about him."

"Things settled down after that," Joshua said, winding down his story. "I heard people saying that they might go after Lieutenant Governor Hutchinson next."

Mama shook her head. "When will this madness stop?"

"When the British leave," Joshua said resolutely.

"Oh, Joshua, that's an extreme opinion," said his mother. "We're British, after all."

"No, Mama, I don't think so. Not anymore. We're Americans, and it's time that the British treated us as equals."

"You may very well be right, Joshua," his father said. "I have heard some of the wisest men in the colonies make such a suggestion."

"You're a man of sound thinking, Papa," challenged Joshua. "Don't you agree?"

Duncan Murray looked from his son to his wife to his daughter. Then he sighed heavily. "Yes, I believe I do agree."

"What does that mean, Papa?" Lizzie asked.

"It means that Sam Adams is right—about some things. He is right that taxation without representation is unjust, and the colonists have good reason to resist. And it means that if the king continues with this course of action, the British Empire itself will be torn apart."

"You are right about that, Papa," Joshua said. "I don't want a war. I don't even want any more street riots. But I do want the colonies to have the freedom they deserve. I believe Sam Adams is the man who will make that happen. I want to be with him when it does."

And the fire in his eyes burned bright and vigorous.

CHAPTER 10

Mischief at the Print Shop

"Mama, I'm hungry."

Mama, Papa, Lizzie, and Joshua all turned to see five-year-old Emmett standing in the doorway.

"Can I have some breakfast?" Emmett asked, twisting the hem of his nightshirt.

"Of course you can," Mama said. "I'll warm some bread for you. I'll just be a few minutes." She turned to the others. "How about the rest of you? Are you hungry?"

Lizzie shrugged, and Joshua shook his head. Neither of them felt like eating yet.

"I'd better eat something before going in to the shop," Papa said. "I'm sure today will be busy."

"Joshua?" Emmett asked as he climbed into a chair next to his brother. "What happened to you?" His brown eyes were wide with questions.

Joshua touched his hand to his face and smeared a streak through the soot. He glanced at his mother, who met his glance with raised eyebrows. "Well, Emmett, I had a very long night. I was trying to stop a fire."

"Did you?"

"No," Joshua said sadly. "I didn't. A building down at the harbor burned last night."

"Mama and Papa were angry when you didn't come home for supper."

"I know. I've told them I'm sorry for worrying them. Everything is going to be fine." He stroked Emmett's head gently.

"Ooh, you're dirty! Don't touch me!"

Everyone laughed.

"Why didn't anyone wake me up?" Olivia burst through the door, rubbing her eyes with one hand.

"It's still early," Lizzie said.

"But everyone else is up. I don't like to be asleep when everyone else is awake." She blinked and looked at her oldest brother. "Joshua, did you fall into the cinder box?" She stuck a finger in his cheek and inspected the soot that rubbed off.

Lizzie and Joshua laughed.

"He was putting out a fire," Emmett said proudly.

"Really?" Olivia's eyes grew wide with excitement. "Are you a hero, Joshua?"

"Hardly. I was just trying to help take care of Boston."

"Heroes do that. Like Sam Adams. You always tell me that Sam Adams is a hero."

Lizzie watched as her father and her brother looked at each other.

"How about some breakfast, Olivia?" Papa said, changing the subject. He swooped her up and set her in a chair.

"Constance, let's slice some more bread. We should all have something to eat."

The bread was soon on the table along with a pot of steaming tea and a chunk of butter. Mama produced some honey and rationed it carefully.

"Mmm. I love bread and honey," Olivia said emphatically, licking her sticky fingers.

"I should probably get to the shop early today," Papa said. "After last night, there will be a lot of activity to report on."

"Like the fire?" Emmett asked.

"Yes, like the fire."

"Are you going to write that Joshua was a hero?" Olivia asked. Her sense of adventure was in full swing.

"I think your hero needs to go clean up," Mama said, giving Joshua a motherly look. "You're getting cinders all over the table."

"Sorry, Mama."

"You should get some rest," Mama said as she looked from Joshua to Lizzie. "Both of you."

Joshua nodded. "I'm exhausted. I'll clean up and go to bed. But don't let me sleep all day. I have some things I need to do this afternoon."

Lizzie wondered what business Joshua had that was so urgent. But to her surprise, neither of her parents pressed Joshua on the point. Lizzie sighed as she watched Joshua leave the room. No doubt Sam Adams was going to hold a meeting of the Sons of Liberty to discuss their activities of the night before, and Joshua planned to be there.

"You should go back to bed, too, Lizzie," Mama urged.

Lizzie shook her head emphatically. "I just know I wouldn't be able to sleep. I want to go to work with Papa."

"I'm not sure that's a good idea today," Mama said. "He'll be very busy."

"That's why I should go. I can help."

"Duncan?" Mama turned to Papa.

He nodded. "It's all right. She'll rest when she's ready. In the meantime, I could use another hand around the shop. She's pretty good with the typesetting." Papa winked at Lizzie.

They did not speak as they rode the carriage from the house to the shop. Merry trotted along cooperatively. She showed no sign that she sensed anything was different about this day. But Lizzie knew that the day was different. Joshua had made a decision from which he would not turn back. Even her parents seemed to recognize that his actions had not been a boyish impulse, but a decision of manhood.

With only two years between their ages, Lizzie and Joshua had played together as small children and watched out for one another as they grew up. They had been inseparable, the way that Olivia and Emmett were constantly together now. But today Joshua had taken a step ahead of Lizzie. He was going to a place where she was not ready to go. And she felt strangely lost without the comfort of his presence.

When they arrived at the print shop, several of the

people who wrote stories for Papa were already out front, eager to give firsthand accounts of the night before. Lizzie could tell just by looking at them that they had been up all night. Although they had cleaned up a bit, they were haggard, and their clothing was not on quite straight. Most of all, they had the same fire in their eyes that she had seen in Joshua's.

Papa unlocked the shop and let the eager writers in. He left Lizzie to get Merry settled until they would need the mare again. Lizzie looped the reins around the post in front of the shop, then stroked Merry's head.

"Did you hear anything last night, girl?" Lizzie asked. "Were you frightened?" Merry nuzzled her hand. Lizzie fished in her pocket and came up with a sugar cube.

"Mama doesn't know I have this. I've been saving it for you." She laughed as the horse took the cube and licked her hand, looking for more. "I have to go inside now. I said I would help, so I'd better get to work."

Lizzie and her father worked peacefully side by side for several hours. Lizzie tried to guess what Papa would need before he needed it—more paper, more ink, a tray of brass molds for setting the type, even a drink of water every now and then. They worked hard, and by lunchtime the day's edition was ready to print. Mama had packed some bread and ham and apples for them, and they allowed themselves a few minutes to relax and enjoy their food.

"Let's get the press going," Papa said, wrapping the remains of their lunch in some old paper.

Lizzie knew what to do next. She reached for the jar of thick black ink and started smearing it on the rows of metal type. Her father dampened some paper, laid it on the inked type, and got ready to bring the weight of the press down on it. He pulled down on the iron bar, and the ink on the rows of type was pressed onto the paper. Lizzie lifted the sample page and held it up for inspection. She ignored the fact that the lead story was about the burning of the effigies the night before. Instead, she simply took pride in the work she had done.

"Perfect!" she said.

Papa nodded. "It looks pretty good. Let's do the rest."

A spray of pebbles hit the window, startling them both. Outside, Merry neighed loudly.

"What's wrong with Merry?" Lizzie asked, losing interest in the sample sheet.

Papa nodded toward the door. "Go check on her."

Lizzie pulled open the shop door and gasped. A group of little boys, not more than nine or ten years old, were gathered around Merry. The horse was obviously distressed by their actions.

"Leave her alone!" Lizzie cried.

"Redcoat!"

"Lobsterback!"

The boys ignored Lizzie and formed a circle around Merry. One threw a rock that bounced off Merry's hoof. The boys laughed as the horse lifted her foot and neighed again.

"Get away!" Lizzie shouted.

"We'll show you that we are not idiots! You cannot treat us like children."

"We have a right to govern ourselves."

"Light the torch!" one of the boys commanded.

"Stop!" Lizzie screamed. This time she forced her way into the circle of boys, pushing two of them off balance. Around Merry's neck hung a paper cutout that was crudely shaped like a man and suspended by clothing lines.

"What do you think you are doing to my horse?" Lizzie demanded.

"Didn't you hear about last night?" one of the boys said. His excitement was obvious. "They burned the stamp distributor."

"They burned something made to look like him," Lizzie corrected. "Mr. Oliver is quite well this morning." In one emphatic motion, she ripped the paper cutout from around Merry's neck and threw it at the boy.

"He deserves to be burned in the flesh," the boy retorted.

"Why would you say such a thing? That's cruel." Lizzie soothed the restless horse with a stroking hand.

"It's what my father says. He was there last night and saw the whole thing. He even got to carry the effigy for part of the time."

Even Lizzie was surprised when a big hand reached into the group of boys and grabbed the shirt of the boy who was speaking.

"Do you think that is something to be proud of?" Papa asked.

Lizzie had not heard her father come out of the shop, but she was glad he was there. She leaned her face against Merry's, receiving as much comfort as she gave. Her eyes darted nervously from boy to boy.

"Sure it is," the boy asserted. "My father is no coward. He is not going to stand around and let King George do whatever he wants with the men in the colonies."

"Young man," Papa said, "I know your father. It is true that he is a free thinker and makes up his own mind about what he believes. No one tells him what to think."

"That's right!" the boy said proudly.

"I suggest that you learn something from your father. You have your own mind, too. Use it to decide what you think. Standing around the street pestering an innocent animal is no act of courage."

The boys looked at him, stunned. Papa looked them in the eyes, one by one.

"Now go on about your business and leave the horse alone," Papa said. The boys scampered away in several directions. Merry calmed down. But Lizzie was still nervous. What if Papa had not come out when he did?

"Thank you, Papa," Lizzie said as they went back into the shop.

"You were doing just fine, Lizzie. You stuck to the facts, and you remembered that cruelty is no virtue."

"It's stupid for a bunch of boys to act like a horse is

a tree!" Lizzie cried. She hated to think what could have happened to Merry if the boys had tried to light the effigy they'd hung around her neck.

"They're just children," Papa reminded her. "They were only imitating what they see and hear adults doing."

Joshua's breakfast account of the night before was still vivid in Lizzie's mind. If those boys had heard their fathers and brothers tell the story, too, then they knew enough details to spend the whole day imitating what they had heard.

"Papa, last night. . .what does all this mean for Boston—for the colonies?"

Papa guided Lizzie to sit in a chair and took one of her hands in his.

"Lizzie, you're growing up, trying to understand things for yourself. That's good."

"But I don't understand," she insisted. "Joshua seems to know everything, but I don't understand why this has to happen."

Papa shook his head. "Sometimes I don't understand, either," he said. "Things are changing. We cannot deny that. Joshua reminds us of that every day. But I can tell you this. Boston will settle down again. The people of this city are proud of what they have accomplished, and they want a good life for their families."

"I'm afraid Joshua will get hurt like that soldier that Uncle Philip took care of."

Papa nodded his understanding. "I worry about that,

too. People are doing things that you and I think are crazy. In his heart, I believe Joshua thinks their actions are crazy, too. But he believes in their purpose. And I respect him for acting on what he believes."

Papa pulled Lizzie to his chest for a long hug. She nestled her face against her father's shoulder, and suddenly her head felt as heavy as a stone.

"Papa?"

"Yes, Lizzie?"

"I'm tired."

Papa chuckled. "You can sleep on the cot in the back room."

Lizzie stumbled into the back room, laid down up on the cot, and immediately gave in to the blackness of her exhaustion.

CHAPTER 11

Rooms for Redcoats

"I always thought you were a fair man, Papa!"

Joshua slumped into a wooden chair and tried to control his frustration. His jaw was set tightly, and he glared at his father through narrowed eyes.

"You may think what you like about me, Joshua, but I have made up my mind." Duncan Murray could be every bit as stubborn as his son. He could remain calm and even-tempered no matter how much Joshua ranted and stormed about the print shop.

Lizzie sat on a stool, listening. She was setting the headline type for that afternoon's edition of the newspaper. Her father and brother seemed to have the same discussion every few days. Lizzie continued working as she listened.

Boston had settled down for a few days after the riot Joshua had witnessed. But there had been other riots. Some of the mobs were more organized than others, but they had all tried to draw attention to their cause by actions that the public could not ignore. Lizzie had seen Daniel Taylor hanging around the street corners with his followers. Daniel had not returned to school when classes resumed in the fall. Apparently, he had decided to devote all of his time to being patriotic.

Joshua went to school and, in the afternoons, helped in the shop, but from time to time he mysteriously disappeared. He never again worried his parents by staying out all night, and he insisted that he thought the violence was wrong. But Lizzie knew that he would often take a detour when he was delivering papers in the afternoon. He wanted to spend a few minutes under the elm tree in the center of town—Sam Adams's Liberty Tree.

Lieutenant Governor Hutchinson's home was invaded, as Joshua had predicted. His furniture had been thrown out the window and the house itself nearly destroyed. He and his family had escaped with only the clothes they wore and what little they could hurriedly gather and carry. While Joshua continued to agree with his parents that the violent actions were wrong, he also continued his friendship with Sam Adams. He believed in the changes Sam wanted to bring to Boston and all the colonies.

"Sam Adams only wants what is fair," Joshua said as he continued his dispute with his father. "Surely you can appreciate that."

"Of course I can," Papa said calmly. "But do you think what the Sons of Liberty did to the Hutchinson house was fair?"

Joshua had no answer.

"Hutchinson publicly opposed the Stamp Act," Papa continued, "but the mob attacked his home and family simply because he is an agent of the government in England. That, I assure you, is not fair."

"The Sons of Liberty were not the only ones involved in that," Joshua argued. "The mob got out of control."

"But who stirred up the mob? It was Adams, I tell you. Hutchinson is chief justice of the superior court, and that mob took away everything he owned. He was right when he said that simple indignation could touch off an uncontrolled emotional frenzy. The indignation may be just; the frenzy is not. The Sons of Liberty are only hurting their own cause by such behavior."

Joshua stood up again and folded his arms across his chest. "But you agree that taxation without representation is not fair, don't you?" he pressed.

"You know that I agree. We have discussed this many times before. The Stamp Act will draw resources out of the colonies. We are being taxed without having a say in the decision for how to use the taxes. That is not fair."

"Then why won't you print this?" Joshua thrust a paper toward his father.

Papa did not take the paper. He had already looked at it closely enough. He turned to the tray of metal letters on the counter next to Lizzie. She watched him expertly pick the letters he needed. "What is written on that paper is inflammatory and lacking in facts. I will not print it." He began setting the letters in the tray he was working on.

"Papa, be reasonable."

"That is exactly what I am trying to do."

Lizzie watched her father work with admiration. She wondered if she would ever be able to set type as fast as he could. Even Joshua's nagging did not distract him.

"What is written on this paper is important to the cause of the colonies. Papa, you have a printing press. Surely you realize what a great help that is to the cause. You can make an important contribution without ever leaving your shop."

"I will not print that article, Joshua." Papa spoke without turning around.

"Then let me do it," Joshua said. "I know how to work the press. I've been helping you for years."

"I will not contribute to the violence, Joshua, even indirectly. I will not stir up the anger of the people so that they go out and destroy property. I do not wish to endanger lives without just cause."

"I'm not asking you to do any of that. I just want to print a few papers."

"Rewrite the article. Then come to me again."

"I can't change the article, Papa. Sam Adams wrote this himself."

"Then ask him to rewrite it."

"I can't do that."

Papa finally turned from his tray of type. "You can do anything you choose to do, Joshua," he said as he looked his son in the eye. "You have already proven that."

Joshua sighed and stuffed the paper into his pocket.

The first time Lizzie had overheard such a discussion, she had been shocked that Joshua would use such a tone with their father. When they were younger, talking back to their parents had been strictly forbidden. She herself would never question her father's authority.

However, after several of these discussions, she knew just how both Joshua and her father would sound. Joshua would plead for his father to be more involved with the cause of the Patriots. Specifically, he thought Papa should use his press to print only literature in favor of the Patriots. He argued that the Loyalists had more than enough support coming from England. But the Patriots had to organize themselves from nothing and make the most with what little aid they could find. Duncan Murray's press could be a precious resource.

Lizzie's father, on the other hand, reserved the right to examine and approve anything that his press was used to print. In the newspaper, he was concerned about being fair. He gave the facts on both sides of any controversy. When everyone else in Boston seemed free with their opinions, Duncan Murray held up the facts and held back his tongue. In fliers and pamphlets, he steadfastly refused to print anything he thought would cause further violence, no matter who had written it.

This infuriated Joshua. If Sam Adams was seeking what was fair for all the colonies, why shouldn't Duncan Murray help?

"It's important that people understand what the Stamp Act Congress is, Papa," Joshua pleaded. "The colonies have to work together to oppose the Stamp Act, and this congress is the way to do that. Will you at least print Sam's article on the congress?"

"I have already printed several articles informing people the congress is taking place," Papa answered.

"I know, Papa, and Sam appreciates that. But the people need more than information about when the congress will happen. They need to understand why it is needed. This will be the first time that all the colonies stand united in one protest against Parliament. This is a new strategy, for the good of the colonies."

"All right." Papa turned back to his typesetting. "Sam Adams may write a piece, and if it is not inflammatory, I will print it."

"Thank you, Papa."

"But," Papa continued, shaking a finger at Joshua, "if someone else chooses to write an article opposing the congress who presents reasonable arguments, I will print that, too."

Joshua sighed. "I suppose that is only fair."

"Good. You see my point at last."

Lizzie was relieved that this one battle seemed to be over.

The shop door opened, and the bell tinkled. Lizzie swung around on her stool to see her uncle Blake enter. He was red in the face and angrier than Lizzie had ever seen him.

"Blake!" Papa exclaimed. "What's going on?"

Uncle Blake waved a paper. "They want Charlotte and me to take in two British soldiers; that's what's going on."

Lizzie hopped off her stool to greet her uncle and pay closer attention to the conversation.

"The Quartering Act," Papa stated flatly.

"Yes, the Quartering Act. Is it my problem that the king's

army cannot provide enough barracks for its own troops? They have brought that upon themselves, if you ask me."

"Let me see the paper," Papa said, reaching for it. He read it closely. "They leave you no option, Blake. You could face severe penalties if you refuse to do this."

Uncle Blake pounded the edge of the printing press. "Charlotte and I are barely finding enough food for the boys and ourselves as it is. How can we possibly stretch our meager rations to feed two more full-grown men?"

"We'll help all we can," Papa assured him.

Lizzie pictured her mother trying to make her precious staples extend to another household.

"You already have six mouths to feed at your house," Uncle Blake retorted. "You haven't got a morsel to spare, and you know it."

"Especially not for a British soldier," Joshua blurted out. "I'll not have my brother's and sisters' food cut back so that a lobsterback can eat well."

"And I would not take a crumb out of their mouths," Uncle Blake assured Joshua. He sighed. "Duncan, I don't know how you keep going. If things do not get better soon, Wallace Coach and Carriage will face serious problems. I hate the thought of closing up the business. I want to give my boys the same legacy my uncle gave me when he left me Wallace Coach."

"And you will, Blake, you will."

"Do you see why we need the congress, Papa?" Joshua said. "Forcing residents of Boston to feed and house British soldiers is just another form of taxation without represen-tation. We have to stop this before it goes any further."

"Listen to the boy, Duncan," Uncle Blake said. "He's absolutely right about this."

"You are in favor of the congress, then?" Joshua asked hopefully.

"Certainly, I am." Uncle Blake was emphatic.

"And you think Sam Adams is right?"

"Sam Adams—and a lot of other people. I know Sam has drummed up a lot of support. He gives talks under the Liberty Tree and organizes the Sons of Liberty. But he is not the only man in Boston thinking this way. The idea of the congress really came from James Otis. It makes a lot of sense to me."

"It's against the law," Papa said. "Any governor who sends representatives will be openly defying the king. The men who attend could be arrested as soon as they return."

"It will be worth that price if the congress accomplishes what James Otis hopes it will," Uncle Blake said.

"That's right!" Joshua exclaimed.

"Not everyone agrees," Papa pointed out. "The gover-nors of Virginia, Maryland, North Carolina, and Georgia have forbidden their representatives to attend."

"That still leaves nine colonies," Uncle Blake said, "a large enough majority to make an impression on the king. And the other governors will no doubt send their own let-ters of protest. We are all suffering because we are boycot-ting British goods. Eventually the boycott will hurt England more than it does us. Then the progress we make will be worth the price we are paying now."

"I am concerned that the Stamp Act Congress will bring more violence to the streets," Papa said.

"The violence will come with or without the congress," Uncle Blake insisted. "When the Stamp Act goes into law in November, madness will follow. But if the people believe in the Stamp Act Congress, if they commit to a reasonable course of action, then perhaps less damage will be done."

"I think Uncle Blake is right," Joshua said. "And what you print can influence people to support the congress and help stop the riots."

Papa smiled faintly as he looked from his son to his brother-in-law. "The two of you are sure thinking alike." Papa handed Uncle Blake the quartering orders. "But none of that changes this command, Blake. It will be unpleasant, but for the sake of your family's safety, you must obey."

Blake shook his head. "If I refuse, I am in danger with the government. If I obey, I am at risk with the mobs. I am not worried about myself or even Charlotte. But I do not want the boys to be caught in the middle of all this."

"Send the boys to stay with us," Lizzie suggested.

"That's a great idea," Papa agreed. "Olivia and Emmett would love it. Just until things settle down."

Lizzie was glad she had made the suggestion. Like her uncle Blake, she hated to think that anything might happen to Isaac or Christopher. Her little cousins would be safer at her house. But would things ever settle down enough for Isaac and Christopher to go home?

CHAPTER 12
Just One Soldier

"They're back!" came the cry.

And suddenly the cobblestone street was filled with activity. Merchants left their shops. Women grabbed their babies and left their homes. Horses and carriages and people on foot gathered in the town square to greet the Boston representatives of the Massachusetts Assembly. They had returned safely from the Stamp Act Congress in New York City, and the whole city of Boston was curious to hear their report.

"Whoa." Lizzie tugged on the reins and pulled Merry to a stop. The afternoon deliveries would be delayed for a few minutes. Without waiting for the cart to stop, Joshua abandoned his newspapers and leaped down from the seat. He ran toward the returning delegation and became part of a crowd clamoring for information. Lizzie did not even try to persuade Joshua to stay with the cart. He had been waiting for this moment so eagerly. For the past few days, he had talked about little but the Stamp Act Congress and how Parliament would respond.

Lizzie decided to stay with Merry, lest any harm come to the old mare in the middle of a crowd. She held the reins tightly in case a sudden movement spooked the horse into action. She could not hear much, but because of the height of the cart, Lizzie could see most of what was happening.

The representatives were tired, dusty, and eager for a hot meal. They would make a complete report later, but the townspeople would not wait for formalities. They wanted their news firsthand and immediately. Those closest to the mounted representatives asked the questions on everyone's mind.

"Did you tell the king to forget about his taxes?"

"Do all the colonies agree?"

"What's next?"

The report was organized soon enough, and word filtered back through the crowd. Nine colonies had sent representatives, and the other four had agreed to abide by the outcome of the congress. The result of the meetings had been a letter to the king declaring certain American rights and listing the complaints of the colonies about the British government's recent actions.

Joshua came whooping out of the crowd. Thrashing with excitement, he pushed his way past a line of human obstacles and hurled himself up into the carriage next to Lizzie.

"Did you hear all that, Lizzie?" he asked.

The fire in his eyes was burning brightly, and he grinned as he had not grinned for weeks. She nodded.

"And do you know what it means?"

Again, Lizzie nodded. Then she said, "But, Joshua, the letter will not reach King George for weeks. The Stamp

Act will be in effect before that."

Joshua took the reins and nudged Merry forward ever so slightly. "That's true. But the congress is about more than just the Stamp Act."

"What do you mean? It's called the Stamp Act Congress."

"But it goes beyond that." Joshua paused to reach back and throw a small bundle of papers to a waiting merchant. He continued. "We're Americans, and we have rights. That's what it is about. The king has to see that we will not stand for the Stamp Act or anything else that does not respect our rights and independence. You see, we aren't simply trying to change the stamp tax. We're trying to change the way the British government looks at the colonies."

"That sounds like an awfully big job to me."

"It is. But the Stamp Act Congress is an important first step."

"And in the meantime?" Lizzie asked, dreading the day the Stamp Act would take effect.

Joshua shrugged. "We live one day at a time and see what each day brings."

Lizzie reached over and pulled on the reins. "You missed a stop. We're still delivering papers, remember?"

"Right." Joshua jumped down. "Help me with these. We leave two stacks at this stop."

Lizzie got down. She could not lift the bound stacks as easily as Joshua could. She often pleaded with him to tie smaller bundles, but he just told her to grow bigger muscles. He was already gone with the first stack. Huffing, she tugged the second stack off the back of the cart and strained to carry it to the shop's door.

"Here, let me help you with that."

Lizzie looked up into the face of a British soldier. Her heart leaped in her throat. Never had a soldier spoken to her before. But this was not just any British soldier. She recognized the clear gray eyes and soft brown hair. This was the young man she had helped care for in Uncle Philip's clinic.

After that day when the soldier had been injured, Lizzie had stopped by the clinic to check on his recovery several times. But she had always spoken with her uncle, never directly with the soldier. She had not seen him at all in the six months since Uncle Philip had declared him fit and sent him back to his regiment.

"I can manage," she muttered, adjusting her load. Her heart pounded. Any second she was sure to drop the newspapers on her foot.

"I insist," he said, and he took the stack from her. "Where do they go?"

She gestured. "Just over there, by the door." Her voice was hardly more than a whisper.

Joshua came out of the shop.

"Hey, what are you doing?" He snatched the papers from the soldier.

"I was just helping your sister." The soldier's response

was calm. "I wanted to repay her kindness of some time ago." He looked down at Lizzie with steady gray eyes. She had looked into those eyes six months ago and seen fear. Now she saw emptiness. Her heart softened as she returned his gaze.

"I appreciated the way you cared for me," the soldier said. "You could have left me to bleed to death."

"I would never have done that." Lizzie did not know how she found the strength to speak. "Besides, it was my uncle who knew what to do."

"All the same, I've been wanting to thank you. But I did not know how to find you."

Joshua finally realized who the young man was. "You're. . .you're better." He let the stack of newspapers drop to the ground several feet off target.

"Yes, I am fully recovered." The soldier turned to look at Joshua. "And I extend my thanks to you, as well."

Lizzie looked at his jacket and saw the crude stitching on one shoulder. Someone inexperienced with a needle and thread had tried to repair the uniform where Uncle Philip had cut it. The soldier looked even more thin and ragged than he had six months ago, if that was possible. Lizzie's heart tightened.

"Are you on duty?" Lizzie asked. He carried no musket.

The soldier glanced around. "I am looking for work."

"Around here?" Lizzie asked. She knew that the merchants in this neighborhood were not likely to be able to pay a hired hand—even if they would agree to hire a

British soldier, which was doubtful.

"The jobs at the docks are all taken," the soldier explained. "I thought it could not hurt to look elsewhere."

"But you have a job. You're a soldier." Joshua spoke with an edge to his voice. Lizzie glared at him. If Joshua would only look at the pitiful state this soldier was in, he would not say such cruel things.

The soldier's voice was low. "I have not been paid in months," he said. "The barracks are crowded. There is not enough food." His voice drifted away.

Lizzie glanced down at the soldier's boots, wondering if he had gotten new ones or if he still filled the holes with layers of newspaper.

"Perhaps we can help you," Lizzie said impulsively.

"Lizzie!" Joshua said in a harsh whisper. "May I speak with you?" Without waiting for an answer, he grabbed her wrist and jerked her back over toward their cart. Merry neighed and swished her tail.

"Have you gone mad? Lizzie, why would you offer to help a British soldier? Have you listened to nothing that I have said in the last few months?"

Lizzie twisted out of her brother's grip. "Of course I've heard you. Every word. You never stop talking about your cause. But have you looked at him, Joshua? Really looked at him?"

Lizzie put a hand on the mare's neck, both to steady herself and to give herself something familiar to concentrate on.

Joshua kept his eyes on Lizzie. "I realize he is having a difficult time. But we all are."

"Don't be silly, Joshua. You must weigh twenty pounds more than he does. Mama makes sure that you eat properly, even in hard times."

"Suppose he were one of the soldiers living in Uncle Blake and Aunt Charlotte's house?" Joshua argued. "Suppose he were one of the ones taking food away from Isaac and Christopher?"

"But he's not!" Lizzie retorted. "And he's hungry and cold just like any human being would be. Look at him, Joshua! Look at him!"

She punched his shoulder until he gave in and turned around. The soldier, not believing that Lizzie would return to help him, was leaning up against the side of the building. In his dejection, all he could do was trace shapes in the dirt with his ragged boots.

"We have to help him, Joshua."

"You're helping the enemy, Lizzie."

"He's not the enemy, Joshua. He's just one soldier. That could be you in a couple of years."

Joshua was silent and swallowed hard. "I don't know, Lizzie, I don't know."

"Why is it so hard for you to see he needs help? He needs us now just as much as that day in Uncle Philip's clinic."

"This is not the same thing."

"Yes, it is. You're always preaching about doing what is fair. Something that is truly fair is fair to everyone, not just to people you agree with. It's not fair that you should have enough to eat, and he does not."

Joshua did not answer.

"If I want to help him, you can't stop me," Lizzie insisted.

"Well, if it isn't Joshua and Lizzie Murray."

A gruff voice from behind surprised them both. Lizzie wheeled around to face Daniel Taylor. Behind him were three of his gang, casually thumping sticks against the palms of their hands.

"I saw you talking to that soldier, Lizzie."

Lizzie tossed her hair back proudly. "So what if I did? It's not any of your business."

"I'll make it my business if I see you talking to him again."

"Don't threaten my sister," Joshua growled.

Daniel turned haughtily to Joshua. "Don't tell me you're turning into a lobsterback, Joshua. I would have thought better of you than that."

Joshua put up his fists. "You mind your own business, Daniel Taylor."

The boys behind Daniel stood poised with their sticks in the air.

Lizzie lurched between Daniel and Joshua and grabbed Joshua's wrists. "What are you doing, Joshua? Fighting won't solve anything."

Daniel laughed. "Ha! Now I know why you say that to me all the time, Joshua. You're taking orders from your little sister."

"I'm not taking orders from anyone!"

"Just don't talk to that soldier again," Daniel said, staring at Lizzie. She stared back at him, her chin in the air and her stomach churning violently.

When Daniel moved on down the street, Lizzie searched for the soldier. He was gone.

CHAPTER 13

Night of Terror

Crash!

Lizzie ran to the front window. Joshua was close behind.

"What was it?" she asked as they leaned against the glass and peered into the street.

"I can't see anything from in here," moaned Joshua. "If Mama and Papa would just let me go out for a few minutes, I could find out what is going on."

Their father spoke behind them. He made no move to get any closer to the window. "Joshua, we discussed this already, and you agreed to stay in."

"But, Papa, I just want to find out what is happening. Aren't you curious?"

Papa shook his head. "This is November 1. The Stamp Act took effect today. We all knew what would happen when this day came."

"You are going to have to report on this in the paper tomorrow. I could write a story for you."

"I have other sources. I see no need to put my son at risk."

Constance Murray came down the stairs. She had been upstairs for more than an hour with Emmett, Olivia, Isaac, and Christopher, trying to settle them down and coax them to sleep.

"I think they've settled at last," she said.

"I don't see how they can sleep with all this noise," Lizzie remarked. There was far too much activity in the street to be able to relax and sleep. She knew she would not sleep a moment all night.

"They are exhausted," her mother said. "I made sure that they played very hard today. I knew the night would be like this." Mama ran her fingers through Lizzie's red curls. "You should try to get some rest, too."

Lizzie shook her head vigorously. "No, I'm sure I couldn't sleep."

"Are you going to stay up all night, Papa?" Joshua asked.

Papa nodded somberly. "A rock thrown off course might break a window. A stray spark would do far more damage."

"I'm a member of the Sons of Liberty now, Papa. I should be with them on a night like this."

"For what purpose?" Papa raised his voice slightly, startling Lizzie. "You are one person, Joshua. You cannot stop the rampage, especially when your fellow Sons of Liberty are very likely at the center of it. Most likely, Sam Adams and his gang have spent the evening in their favorite tavern. Now they are so full of ale they have lost their common sense."

"Papa!" Joshua protested. "You can't possibly know that for sure."

"You and I both know that it has happened before.

People have gotten hurt because of a gang's drunken street brawl."

"That is not Sam's purpose."

"No, but it has happened. I have no doubt that the taverns of Boston have seen a lot of business tonight."

"It's a protest, Papa, against an unfair law," Joshua insisted.

"It's madness, Joshua, plain and simple. The king is across the ocean, no doubt enjoying a fine breakfast right now. These riots mean nothing to him."

"Oh, Papa!"

"Joshua," Papa warned. "I don't want to hear another word about it. You are forbidden to go out tonight."

Joshua flung himself into a chair to sulk. Papa picked up an iron poke and stirred the fire. The flames danced and cast an orange glow on the room. Mama stood behind Papa and rubbed his shoulders.

"Mama!" came a cry from upstairs.

Mama sighed. "That's Olivia. I guess she's still awake after all."

"I'll go," Lizzie said and turned to the stairs. She welcomed a reason to escape the tension in the front room. The disagreements between her father and her brother were almost as difficult to listen to as the ruckus outside.

Upstairs, she crept into the room she shared with Olivia. "I'm here, Olivia," she said softly.

"I can't sleep," the little girl said as she rubbed her eyes with her fists.

Lizzie sat on the bed next to her sister. "I know. But you must try. I'll stay with you until you fall asleep."

Olivia pulled the bedding up under her chin and rolled toward the wall. *Our mother is right,* Lizzie thought. *Olivia is exhausted.* Gently, she rubbed her little sister's back to soothe her.

The street noise was muffled on the second floor of the house. Lizzie could still sense that the neighborhood was active, but she could not make out the sounds. Nevertheless, she could not relax. Without a fire and her parents in the room with her, she felt even more on edge. She was isolated, alone. Even as she tried to bring comfort to Olivia, her own fear grew.

In the dim moonlight that filtered through the window, Lizzie studied Olivia's face. In her sleep, Olivia looked far less overwhelming than she was when awake. She was a boisterous child, always seeking adventure. She could hardly sit still for more than three minutes at a time. In many ways, Olivia was like Joshua. They were natural leaders, not afraid to say what they thought. People enjoyed being around them and paid attention to what they did.

If Olivia were older, she would probably have the same fire for the colonists' cause that Joshua had. Lizzie was glad Olivia was too young to get involved in the controversy between England and the colonies. Lizzie sincerely hoped that by the time Olivia was Joshua's age, the debate would be long over. Surely in ten years, life in Boston would once again be comfortable and peaceful.

At last Olivia's breathing was even and deep. Lizzie crept from the room and down the stairs. Joshua had scooted his chair closer to the window, and her parents had sat down together. No one was speaking.

Even though Joshua was grouchy and complained about having to stay in, Lizzie was glad their parents had forbidden him to go out. Joshua thought he was grown-up enough to make his own decisions, but Lizzie was glad to have someone looking out for him. At least she would not have to spend the night worrying about his safety.

Lizzie returned to her post beside Joshua at the window. Outside, a steady stream of people rushed through the streets, some with torches. *Are the torches to give light or to set fire to something?* Lizzie shuddered at the thought of more fires erupting in Boston.

Papa was right: This was more than a crowd protesting an unfair law. It was a mob determined to find revenge. People were running in every direction. Men swung their guns around in the air. Boys not much older than Joshua were out there, standing below the windows of Loyalists, shouting names and throwing rocks. The Stamp Act Congress had brought hope for a few weeks—hope that the law would be short-lived once King George received the protest of the colonies. But her father was right. They all had known that Boston would explode in fury on the day that the law took effect. Now they watched out the window to learn how vicious the fury was.

"Lizzie, come sit with us," her mother invited. "You've

been feeling poorly. I don't want you to catch a chill standing by the window."

"Joshua can watch out the window for all of us," her father said.

Joshua raised his eyes to give his parents a dejected glance.

"Come, Lizzie." Mama raised one arm to welcome her daughter.

Lizzie snuggled in next to her mother. She shivered despite the roaring fire.

"You're safe here, Lizzie," her mother said in low, soothing tones.

As Lizzie leaned her head against her mother's shoulder, she felt the welcome weight of a quilt spread over her. The fire was the only light in the room. It snapped and crackled, mesmerizing Lizzie. Despite her earlier protests, Lizzie gave way to her exhaustion and slept.

The pounding on the door woke her up.

She threw off the quilt and sprang to her feet. "What is it?" she cried. *How long have I been asleep? Why am I in the front room and not in my bed?* The disorientation cleared, and she remembered the events of the evening. Blinking her eyes, she saw that it was still dark outside the window.

Mama pulled Lizzie back as Joshua and Papa went to the door. The pounding came again.

"Who is there?" Papa demanded. With one hand, he double-checked the bolt on the door.

"We need to see Joshua!" came the gruff reply.

"I demand that you tell me who you are," Papa insisted.

"Just open the door!"

"That's Daniel Taylor!" Lizzie exclaimed.

Papa looked at Joshua, who nodded. "She's right. I'm sure that's his voice." He looked out the window, then said, "There are seven or eight boys out there. They look mad."

"I know he used to be a friend of yours," Papa said to Joshua. "Have you had anything to do with him recently?"

"No, Papa! I have seen him in the streets, but he is not one of my friends any longer."

Papa turned back to the door. "What business do you have here?" he shouted through the bolted door.

"My business is with Joshua—and Lizzie."

"Me?" Lizzie cried. "I have nothing to do with Daniel Taylor." Her mind flashed back to the scene in the street, when Daniel had thwarted her determination to help a hungry soldier.

A spray of rocks pelted the front door. Lizzie clutched her mother's arm.

"Please leave!" Papa shouted.

"No rocks!" Daniel screamed at his companions. He turned back to the door. "I promise you no harm will come to you, Mr. Murray. I simply want to speak with Joshua and Lizzie."

Father glared at Joshua. "What have you been up to, Joshua? Why does Daniel Taylor want to speak to you? And have you gotten Lizzie involved in your inflammatory behavior?"

125

"Papa, no!" Joshua said adamantly. "Daniel and his gang are on their own. I promise you I have had no dealings with them."

"Then why does he want to see you so badly?"

"I don't know. Truly, I don't know."

Papa turned back to the door. "Send your companions away, Daniel. You may speak to Joshua alone."

Lizzie held her breath. Her father was not about to unbolt the door and give entrance to a gang, but would he allow Daniel to come in?

Grunts and scuffles followed.

Joshua watched at the window and reported, "They're going. They've backed up into the street. Everybody but Daniel."

"Does he have a weapon?" Papa asked.

Joshua shook his head. "Not that I can see. He carries only a torch. . .and some sort of bundle."

"My friends have gone, Mr. Murray," Daniel shouted, "but if you do not open the door, I will call them back and we will break it down!"

"He means what he says, Papa," Joshua said.

Papa pointed at a spot on the floor about ten feet from the door. "Stand there, Joshua. This hooligan will not enter our home. He may speak to you from the doorway."

Then Papa wedged one foot against the door, unbolted it, and opened it about twelve inches. "You may speak."

Lizzie could see Daniel's face, darkened with the grime of the night's riot.

"I have something you may be interested in," Daniel said. His nostrils flared as he sneered at Joshua and threw his bundle into the house.

It landed at Joshua's feet and fell open.

"A redcoat's jacket?" Joshua asked.

Lizzie gasped. She could think of only one reason why Daniel Taylor would bring them a soldier's uniform. She broke from her mother and scrambled to get the jacket.

Daniel laughed outside the door. "I thought you would be interested in that!"

Ignoring him, Lizzie held the jacket up for inspection. On one shoulder were the crude stitches she was looking for. She knew who the jacket belonged to.

"Where did you get this?" she demanded.

"Where do you think?" Daniel answered. "I took it off the back of your friend."

"What is he talking about?" Mama demanded. "What have you to do with a British soldier?"

Lizzie barely glanced at her mother. She had no time to explain now.

"Why did you take his jacket?" Lizzie hissed at Daniel. She clutched the dirty jacket to her chest and determined to hold back the tears.

"He won't be needing it anymore." Daniel roared with laughter again.

At that moment, Lizzie loathed Daniel Taylor. She swallowed the lump in her throat, but she could not stop the tears any longer. "You killed him, didn't you?"

Daniel shrugged. "No, I didn't kill him. I just found him that way. So you see? All your tender care was for nothing. You should have let him bleed to death six months ago."

"That's enough!" Papa said, and he shoved the door closed and bolted it.

They could hear the whole gang laughing as Daniel rejoined them in the street.

Lizzie fell to her knees and sobbed.

CHAPTER 14

The Accident

Christmas came that year just as it did every year. The riot that had broken out when the stamp tax took effect had subsided into a series of minor skirmishes. Sam Adams rallied the young men of Boston even more vigorously. Some people flatly refused to buy the little blue stamps for their legal documents. This made doing business very difficult.

Finally, in late December, Boston settled down to a peaceful observance of the Christmas holiday.

Lizzie set the table meticulously, as she did every year. Once again, Uncle Philip, Aunt Johanna, and Charity would share Christmas dinner with the Murrays, along with Uncle Blake and Aunt Charlotte and their two boys. But this year, even having the family together added to the tension.

Uncle Blake had become quite outspoken about his Patriot leanings. If Uncle Blake was doing something dangerous—well, Lizzie did not want to know about it. Many of the Patriots in Boston were disobeying British laws, especially if the law was about money. Joshua considered such defiance to be a patriotic act. He was still sure Uncle Blake was avoiding tax fees.

Uncle Philip was equally emphatic about his tendency

to agree with the Loyalists. He still thought of himself as British, unlike Joshua, who considered himself an "American." Although Uncle Philip had never been to England and probably never would travel there, he trusted England to govern the colonies in a fair way. He argued that the colonies would not have developed as rapidly as they had without the aid of England. It was only right that the colonies should help the mother country when she needed them.

Lizzie's parents tried to continue their neutral stance, but they received constant pressure from both sides. And of course, Joshua's agitation grew every day. Lizzie's heart was heavy when it ought to have been full of joy.

She set the last goblet in its place.

"A beautiful table once again," Aunt Johanna said.

Lizzie smiled as earnestly as she could. "Thank you."

"You do such a lovely job. It's always wonderful to see these beautiful dishes."

"Especially when it's hard to have a real Christmas dinner right now," Lizzie said.

Aunt Johanna's smile faded. "Yes, it's difficult. The food will be simple this year, with no delicacies. But we are all together and all safe. That is what is most important."

Lizzie nodded. "I want to try to make this a nice holiday for Olivia and Emmett. I want them to have wonderful memories of family holidays, even without fancy food."

Aunt Johanna chuckled. "They don't like to eat fancy food, anyway."

Lizzie smiled, this time sincerely. "You're right about that. But they do like to play in the snow." Her face brightened as she tucked a chair under the table. "I think I'll take all the children outside. We can throw snowballs and pull the sled around."

"That's a wonderful idea. I'll help you get them bundled up."

"Ahh!" Olivia stuck her tongue out to catch snow flurries. With her arms stretched out wide, she spun around in circles until she tripped over her own feet and collapsed in the snow. Her brother and her cousins followed her lead.

Lizzie laughed at the sight of the five children, from six to nine years old, sprawled in the powdery snow with their tongues hanging out. It felt good to laugh.

"This is fun!" Emmett, the youngest, exclaimed joyously.

"You said we could play on the sled," Olivia reminded Lizzie.

"We want the sled!" Christopher joined in.

Soon all five were repeating the refrain. "We want the sled. We want the sled."

"All right, all right, we'll get the sled." Lizzie happily gave in to the pressure. She trudged back toward the house and took the sled off its hook. Glancing through a window, she saw Joshua sitting with his uncles. Clearly he considered himself one of the adults. He had far too much on his mind to romp in the snow with children. Lizzie missed the old Joshua, the one who would have been outside acting sillier than all the other children put together.

Lizzie dropped the sled solidly in the snow.

"Me first! Me first!" the children all seemed to say.

One by one, Lizzie dragged the five children in a wide circle around the backyard. The other four clamored behind, throwing snowballs at each other. Seeing their faces and sensing their excitement, Lizzie felt better than she had while setting the table. These children had not taken up sides as either Patriots or Loyalists. They were just children, cousins who enjoyed playing together. She hoped that moments like this one would form their strongest memories.

But she was exhausted. After five trips around the yard, trudging through the snow as fast as she could, Lizzie pleaded for a chance to rest. Then she would give everyone a second turn.

"You play by yourselves," she said. "The older ones can pull the younger ones."

"And then you'll pull us again?" Olivia wanted to be sure the fun was not over.

"I promise. Just let me sit down for a few minutes." Lizzie collapsed on the back stoop outside the kitchen and watched as the children continued to streak through the snow with the sled. They squabbled about who would get to ride in front of the sled and which direction to go. But Lizzie welcomed these signs of normal childhood behavior and did not interfere. Perhaps by next Christmas the stamp tax controversy would be over. Boston would settle down again, and the children would indeed have normal childhoods.

Gradually the children drifted farther and farther back

into the yard. Now only the highest pitches of their conversation reached Lizzie's ears. She had nearly regained her energy, and she thought that at the next sign of a quarrel, she would take over pulling the sled again.

Lizzie looked up to see Olivia pulling the sled up the hill at the back of the yard.

"Wait, Olivia!" she called. The hill that divided the Murray property from the neighbors' was not high, but it was steep. Olivia had never before gone down that hill by herself on a sled. Lizzie jumped to her feet and pushed her way through the snow. Instinct told Lizzie that she should ride down with Olivia.

But Olivia was too far ahead of Lizzie and had much more energy. Before Lizzie was halfway up the hill, Olivia had seated herself on the sled.

"Push me!" Olivia demanded. And her cousin Isaac obeyed.

"No, Olivia!" Lizzie shouted. "Stop!"

But she knew Olivia could not stop the sled once it was in motion. She held her breath and watched. Olivia squealed with delight as she whizzed past Lizzie on her way down.

Suddenly, the sled's left blade hit a rock hidden in the snow. Olivia tumbled off. Lizzie screamed as she saw her little sister land on her head while the sled bumped on down the hill.

"Olivia!"

The little girl did not move. Lizzie felt as if time had stopped. The snow felt like iron weights around her ankles.

She could not make her feet move fast enough. The other children were scattered around the yard, and they stood still, too stunned to move.

"Olivia! Are you all right?" Lizzie called out. No answer came. Finally, she reached the girl. Olivia's eyes were closed, and she lay still. Her chubby face, usually rosy, looked pale against the snow.

Lizzie frantically looked around the yard to spot the child nearest the house. "Christopher!" she shouted. "Go get Uncle Philip! Tell him to come quickly."

Fortunately, Christopher unfroze and ran into the house.

Lizzie laid her hand against Olivia's face and called her sister's name again. Olivia's arms and legs were sprawled in every direction. With all the thick clothing she was wearing, it was difficult to tell whether any of her bones might have been broken in the tumble. Lizzie was afraid to touch her or try to move her. Lizzie looked toward the back of the house. There was no sign of anyone coming to help.

"Uncle Philip!" she screamed. She turned to Emmett. "Emmett, go check and see if Christopher found Uncle Philip. Hurry!"

Obediently Emmett scrambled through the snow toward the house.

"Olivia," Lizzie pleaded, "wake up." Lizzie groped for Olivia's wrist and tried to find a pulse, as she had seen her uncle do with his patients. But she did not really know what she was doing, and when she could not find the pulse, her panic deepened.

A hand on her shoulder made her jump.

"It's all right, Lizzie, I'm here." Uncle Philip knelt in the snow and examined Olivia.

"She landed on her head, Uncle Philip," Lizzie explained. "She won't wake up. I think she broke her neck."

Uncle Philip shook his head. "No, her neck is fine. I don't think anything is broken. Her pulse is a little fast, but she's just been knocked unconscious by the fall."

"Are you sure?"

"Quite sure. I'll take her in the house. You bring the other children."

Uncle Philip gathered Olivia, unconscious, into his strong arms and carried her toward the house.

"Please, God," Lizzie said as the tears began to come, "please let Olivia be all right."

By the time Uncle Philip laid Olivia on a quilt in front of the fire, she was beginning to moan. The whole family was gathered around.

"What. . .happened?" Olivia asked weakly as her eyes fluttered open.

"You took a spill in the snow," Uncle Philip said.

Olivia smiled. "I went down the hill by myself."

"Yes, you did," her uncle said softly.

Constance Murray pushed past her brother to check on her daughter for herself. "We'll talk about that later, Olivia," she said sternly. But her voice also held relief.

Across the room, Lizzie leaned against the wall with her own relief. Olivia could have been seriously hurt, but all she cared about was that she had gone down the hill by herself. Yes, Olivia was all right.

"She'll be fine, Lizzie." Aunt Johanna had come to stand beside her.

Lizzie nodded. "I know." She sighed. "I should have been watching her more carefully."

"No one is blaming you for the accident."

"I should have known she would try something like this," Lizzie insisted. "She's been like this since she was a baby. She has no sense of what might be dangerous."

"Lizzie, you cannot watch everyone every minute of every day."

Lizzie choked back a sob. "I know—especially not Olivia. She gets into too many things."

"That's right." Aunt Johanna chuckled. "She's a very determined child. But you must realize that this was simply a childhood accident. It could have happened to any of the children."

Lizzie glanced at the other children gathered around Olivia. Charity and Christopher were teasing her. And Olivia was already planning her next attack on the hill.

"As I recall," Aunt Johanna said, "something like this happened to you when you were younger."

Lizzie smiled through her tears and nodded. "When I was five, I made wings out of paper from Papa's shop and thought I could fly. I nearly broke my arm when I jumped off a stack of papers in the back of the cart." She shivered. She had not even noticed that she was cold.

"That's right," Aunt Johanna said. "Now, why don't you take that wet cloak off? You're dripping all over the floor."

Lizzie surrendered to her aunt's attempt to remove the soaked clothing. "Aunt Johanna, in a way I'm glad this happened."

Her aunt raised her eyebrows.

"I've been so worried," Lizzie explained, "that Joshua would get hurt, or someone would get angry at Papa for what he prints, or that there would be a war. You kept telling me that God is in charge of all those things."

"That's right," Aunt Johanna said, not quite understanding what Lizzie was getting at.

"Olivia could have been badly hurt, and it had nothing to do with the stamp tax or Parliament or anything. It was just a sled ride. God is in charge of things like that, too."

Aunt Johanna smiled.

"This doesn't mean that we shouldn't be sensible," Lizzie went on seriously. "I shouldn't have jumped off that cart, and Olivia shouldn't have gone down that hill. And I still think that Joshua should stay away from the riots," Lizzie said emphatically. "But no matter what happens, God cares about us. And that's what matters most of all."

Lizzie shuddered and wrapped her arms around herself. "I guess I got wetter than I realized. I think I'll go change my clothes."

And she left her aunt standing in the hall with a satisfied smile on her face.

CHAPTER 15

Victory!

Spring came sweetly in 1766. The rumblings of the Patriots and the retorts of the Loyalists did not interrupt nature's rhythm. The winds warmed, the rains came, the trees budded, and the hills and meadows around Boston were lush and thick once again.

Joshua and Lizzie sat next to each other on the seat in front of the cart on an afternoon in the middle of May. They did not talk. They had finished their rounds with the afternoon's papers, and they were hungry and tired. Their last stop would be back at the print shop to pick up their father and go home for supper.

Lizzie was thirteen now, almost fourteen, and Joshua had passed his sixteenth birthday. Brother and sister did not always agree with each other, but they understood each other well. Joshua respected his parents. He would never do something that he knew would hurt any of his relatives. Lizzie was certain of that. But his decisions were his own now. Somehow the stamp tax controversy had moved Joshua from boyhood to manhood. Lizzie had watched the gulf between her and her brother widen and wondered if she and Joshua would ever find their way back to each other.

Lizzie no longer yearned for life to go back to the way it

was before Parliament began imposing so many restrictions on the colonies. She felt better now than she had a year ago. She was still not sure that she agreed with Joshua's choice of friends. In the last two years, she had witnessed people doing many wild things. But she knew Joshua was right about one thing: Change was coming, and no one would be able to stop it—not even the king of England himself.

Merry trotted along steadily, just as she had for many years. Lizzie swayed with the rhythmic *clip-clop, clip-clop*. Merry was a good horse, a calm, gentle, reliable work partner. With sadness in her heart, Lizzie calculated the mare's age. Even Merry would not be with them much longer. Her father had already remarked several times that they ought to be looking around for another work animal and let Merry live out her old age in peace.

Joshua halted the cart. They were back at the shop. No doubt their father would be wiping down the counters one last time before locking up. The day's work was done for all of them. They would soon relish some rest and nourishment in the family home.

Lizzie pushed the door open and the bell tinkled.

"Papa? Are you ready?"

"I'll just be a minute. Did you have any trouble today?" Duncan Murray had asked his daughter that question every day for months—ever since her encounter with Daniel Taylor during the route so many months ago.

"No, Papa. Everything was fine."

The bell tinkled again and Lizzie turned, expecting to

see Joshua impatient to go home. Instead it was her uncle Blake, with Joshua right behind him.

"We did it!" shouted Joshua gleefully. He pushed past his uncle and grabbed Lizzie's hands, pulling her off balance.

"Did what?" Lizzie asked. She broke from Joshua and steadied herself against the counter.

"What has happened?" Papa asked, tossing aside his rag.

Blake slapped the back of a chair happily. "I've just come from the harbor. A boat came in from England today. The word is that King George has repealed the Stamp Act. He did it on March 18, and Parliament voted to approve it. But the letter only came today."

Joshua clucked his tongue. "I wish there were a faster way to exchange information between England and America."

"Are you sure?" Papa pressed.

"Absolutely! I saw the letter myself."

"Isn't this incredible?" said Joshua, nearly dancing around the room. Lizzie stepped out of his way. "We've done it, we've done it. The congress worked!"

"Lizzie, quick!" Papa said. "We'll do a special announcement and get it out on the streets tonight. Get the letter trays out."

Lizzie flew into action. Her father had just finished cleaning up the day's work. Everything was neatly put away. A moment ago they were ready to go home for supper. But everything had changed in that moment.

"What will the headline be, Papa?" she asked as she pulled out a tray of headline letters.

"King Repeals Stamp Act!" Papa answered.

"No," said Joshua. "Americans Defeat King!"

Papa laughed. "All right, Joshua, have it your way."

"What about supper?" Lizzie asked as she picked out the letters to spell *Americans*. "Mama is expecting us home any minute."

Papa turned to Uncle Blake and raised his eyebrows.

"Don't worry," Uncle Blake said, grinning. "I'll go by the house and tell her the news myself."

"Thank you, Blake. We may not be home for several more hours."

"Before I leave, I must tell you one more thing."

"What's that?"

"Along with the letter of repeal came a new act from Parliament."

Joshua groaned. "Have they learned nothing?"

Uncle Blake shook his head. "Apparently not. This one is called the Declaratory Act."

"What does it say?"

"It asserts Britain's ownership and control over the colonies. I can promise you that Sam Adams and James Otis are not going to like it."

"The work of the Sons of Liberty is not over," Joshua declared. "It's just beginning."

"Can you get us a copy of the act?" Papa asked Uncle Blake.

"I'm sure I can. After I see Constance, I'll run back over to the harbor."

"We greatly appreciate your help, Blake."

"I'll be back as soon as I can." And Uncle Blake was gone.

Papa rubbed his hands together energetically. "Let's get to work! Joshua, get the press ready. Use fresh ink. Lizzie, let's decide what this announcement should say."

"Papa, you relax. Let us do this," Joshua said. "We know what to do."

Lizzie watched the exchange between her father and her brother. Joshua was serious. He wanted the responsibility of getting out this special edition. Papa studied his son's expression for a moment, then nodded.

"All right. You write up the story and let me check it. Then I'll help Lizzie with the typesetting, and you can print it."

"Papa, thank you! You can trust me."

"I can see everything is in good hands," Papa said. "I believe I'll use this opportunity to catch up on some accounts in the back room."

When their father was gone, Joshua grinned at Lizzie.

"I'm glad you got what you wanted," she said.

"It's not just what I wanted," he corrected. "It's what is best for the colonies—for America."

"The way you say that, it sounds as if you think of the colonies as a separate country."

Joshua nodded. "There are some who think that way. But the Declaratory Act means that there is still a lot of work ahead of us if we are to make Parliament see things from our point of view." He picked up a quill and dipped it in ink. "Enough chatter. I must write my story."

Lizzie smiled at his seriousness as he began to scratch on the paper. He was not imitating anyone. This was Joshua being himself, working hard on something he believed in.

Joshua was probably right. Change was coming. The colonies and Britain would have to establish a new relationship. The change would affect even ordinary people on both sides of the Atlantic.

Lizzie found the last letter of her headline: AMERICANS DEFEAT KING! As she read the words, spelled out in front of her on the counter, she felt their impact. The Loyalists in Boston would not like this headline. But Lizzie did. It put words on the fire she had seen glowing in her brother's eyes.

Lizzie Murray was ready to face the change. And she and Joshua would find their bond once again.

If you enjoyed

Lizzie
and the Redcoat

be sure to read other

SISTERS IN TIME

books from BARBOUR PUBLISHING

- Perfect for Girls Ages Eight to Twelve

- History and Faith in Intriguing Stories

- Lead Character Overcomes Personal Challenge

- Covers Seventeenth to Twentieth Centuries

- Collectible Series of 24 Titles

6" x 8¼" / Paperback / 144 pages / $4.97

AVAILABLE WHEREVER CHRISTIAN BOOKS ARE SOLD